Who was he?

Allen Sibley wanted to be a hero. All his life this shrinking little man had connived and maneuvered brilliantly in the corrupt business world—and all his life he had wanted to be different, a man of action, direct and sure.

So when circumstances forced him to do it, he took a new name—Sullivan—and bought himself a new body: big, strong and healthy.

And then he gradually learned that he had a new mind—which was neither Sibley's nor Sullivan's.

By A. J. Budrys

FALSE NIGHT

MAN OF EARTH

This is an original novel—not a reprint—published by
BALLANTINE BOOKS, INC.

MAN OF EARTH

by

A. J. Budrys

BALLANTINE BOOKS   •   NEW YORK

To:

James and Virginia Blish,
for encouraging the competition.

Library of Congress Catalog Card No. 58-8259
Printed in the United States of America

BALLANTINE BOOKS, INC., 101 Fifth Avenue, New York 3, N. Y.

I

DECEMBER, 2197, in New York City, and Allen Sibley slowly turned the corner of a big gray building for the second time. He walked head down, his eyes darting up now and then to search over the passersby for anyone who might have noticed him coming this same way ten minutes before. Embarrassed, he dropped his glance whenever it accidentally touched someone else's, and those people looked at him curiously for a moment before twitching their eyes away and going on about their business.

It was late afternoon—about four o'clock—and the skies were the color of cast iron above the heavy downtown office buildings. He had been walking for the better part of an hour, all the way from his own offices, through the steadily narrowing streets, leaving behind the formal landscaping of the uptown boulevards and the delicate flight of the pedestrian walks above the softly humming roadways. Down here, he found bluff walls and broken sidewalks, soot and, sometimes, cobblestones. Mechanically crossing one street after another, feeling more and more conspicuous in his Moreley Freres surtout among these crowds, he made his way.

From time to time he reached up and touched the edge of the business card in the breast pocket of his surtout. But he never went so far as to take the card out. He knew the address on it. He touched it only to reassure himself it was still there, and to scrape the raw edge of his soul.

As he walked, he saw himself clearly in his mind's uncompromising eye: a pitiful spectacle of a soft, middle-aged but childishly sensitive, irresolute man, who had never in his life been essentially anything else. He knew he was hesitant, indrawn, unable to make up his mind, a proper object for amused contempt. He knew himself thoroughly. He knew that anyone else could see what he was at a glance. He was an incompetent weakling, congenitally fearful, and completely lacking in the pride and strength that distinguished real men from inferior botches like himself. He knew he had only one positive quality: a mind that never stopped thinking, and that constantly thought things like this.

He turned the next corner and found himself again in front of the building's entrance. He stopped and touched the business card once again. And then, with a stolen look around to see if anyone was watching his indecision, he dropped his hand and turned away again, to round the next corner and walk farther, once more around the block.

He knew he should have gone in. He had come down to this neighborhood on the crest of that decision, only to have it break away beneath him when he actually faced the entrance with its tier of company name plates. So now he walked around and around the block, not going in and not going away, not going back to his own offices to sit behind his desk, facing the door and waiting.

He reached up to the card again, his fingers hesitant. It was a terribly frail straw. He forced his legs to carry him forward, and his other arm swung stiffly at his side, out of rhythm with his footsteps. He dropped his hand and walked on. How many years, now? Five? Six?

Six, he thought. The lounge of the Fieldstone Club had been a quiet, hushed place. An occasional servitor moved soundlessly across the Bokhara carpets, carrying a tray;

and every so often members came in or got up and left, some going into the dining room when whispering attendants informed them their luncheon was ready, others going back to their offices, and all stepping quietly. In the high-ceilinged room, with its draperies cutting shafts from the golden sunlight in the windows, their movements back and forth took on a complex rhythm that Sibley caught from the corners of his eyes as he sat reading his newspaper. He held the paper up stiffly before his face, but as the time passed he relaxed a little, lulled by the soft movement in the room and the tang of excellent food still lingering on his palate. He did not wish to speak to anyone, did not wish to so much as nod to an acquaintance; he wanted only this half hour in which to rest, relax and let the accumulated tension of a morning's business seep out of him before he had to return to the business of the afternoon. But while his hands slowly loosened their grip on the paper, his arms drooping down until he was holding it more naturally, he felt a little pang that none of the other members had even tried to penetrate his barrier. He wondered what they thought of him—whether they thought so little of him that the least discouragement was enough to quench any obligation they might feel to politeness.

His mouth moved in hurt sadness. Then he caught himself, and the careful mask of preoccupation settled back on his features. He turned the page, taking care to do it quietly, and went on with his half-reading, not absorbing anything of what his eyes passed over, since he had now turned to the financial page and the figures in it were two hours behind the tapes in his own office.

"Mr. Sibley?"

He looked sideward, caught off guard. He twisted uncomfortably in his chair, his surtout pressed down by one thigh, caught and hampering his body. "Yes?"

Strangers who spoke unexpectedly had always startled him.

The man sitting in the next chair had a round face with plain hair and features that left nowhere for a description to begin. He murmured a name as anonymous as his face, and Sibley was never able to remember it. He held out a white slip of a business card.

"Pardon me for intruding, Mr. Sibley," he said in a voice that seemed to drift toward Sibley and dissipate as soon as it had registered on his ears. "I represent Doncaster Industrial Linens, and your name has been brought to our attention." He moved the card forward, and Sibley found himself reaching up and closing his fingers on it almost unthinkingly, so much in harmony was it with the lounge's slow rhythm of motion, and so unobtrusive the man's manner. It was only when Sibley's fingers closed over the card that he realized he'd actually taken it. He looked down at it uncomfortably, trying to think what to say.

He realized he ought to hand the card back firmly, saying "My dear sir, this is a private club. I do not wish to discuss business here. Furthermore, I have no conceivable use for the services of an industrial laundry. Good day!" But he did not say it. He mumbled:

"But, I don't see . . ."

"Of course, Mr. Sibley," the man said. "You don't see why our firm should intrude on your privacy."

"I—well, no, that's really all right," Sibley answered, instantly embarrassed. "It's just that this *is* a private club . . . some of the other members might object . . ."

"I understand completely, Mr. Sibley. I won't take more than a moment of your time."

"No, no—that's all right, really. I didn't mean . . ." He swallowed the remainder of the sentence at the suspicion of amused scorn in the man's eyes. He looked down at the business card, in confusion at the neat way he'd been out-maneuvered.

"I think it would be best," the man was saying, "if I explained the nature of our firm's service." He looked sharply at Sibley, and said, "Don't you think so?" while nodding.

Sibley nodded and said, "Yes," in reflex.

"We live in a society that has turned in upon itself," the man proceeded at once. "The technological achievements of the twentieth and twenty-first centuries came to an end only after they had reached their logical zenith —the establishment of a state of affairs in which man can produce more than he can possibly consume." The man gestured graciously at the trappings of the room in which they were sitting. "In our time," he commented with gentle redundancy, "we live in luxurious comfort because we have what might be called a stockpile of technology. The techniques of the previous two centuries are entirely adequate for meeting the needs of this one. None of us, I think, need worry unduly about food, clothing, or shelter. That is our treasure, and our cross.

"For the day is coming, Mr. Sibley, when this warm paradise will come to an end. And I think all of us know it, though few of us will admit it. We are rich, but we will be poor. Some day, in the not too distant future, our wonderful technology will have stripped this planet. We will have taken too much. We will have robbed our world—the only world in this solar system on which man may live in any degree of comfort—and it will starve us into pestilence and savagery for its revenge. We know it. But it's so pleasant to sit here. So comfortable. People love comfort, Mr. Sibley. Comfort and luxury. Once they have it, they will not give it up too easily. Even though they know that some day they will lose it.

9

Even though they realize that the more luxury they enjoy today, the sooner the day of reckoning.

"So I think all of us are divided within ourselves, Mr. Sibley. We barricade our fear behind a complex social code, and we scheme and struggle endlessly to preserve what is ours and to take from others what belongs to them so we may add it to our own possessions. We are hoarding against tomorrow's famine, each trying desperately to be the man who will keep his comfort longest—and yet we know that the better we succeed the surer we must die."

The man raised a hand. "Wait, Mr. Sibley. I know. It will be generations, still, before we feel the first pinch. All of us here will be dust by then, and we will all go comfortably into our soft caskets. But neither you nor I can dissociate ourselves from the race of man, and it is the surging racial instinct that has swept us all up. You, and I, and everyone—we fought the cold in icebound caves, once, long ago. We fled from the wolf and slew the bison, and chipped our flints on the banks of rivers that drowned us in flood and parched us in the drought. We *know*, Mr. Sibley—you and I, and everyone here— we *know* the winter is coming."

The man's mood changed abruptly as he finished, much as if an organist had changed stops. He became brisk, urbane, businesslike:

"Naturally, the strain on all of us is very great. In spite of the MacDonnel drive and the little colonies of Venus and Pluto—because of them, I should say, since they *are* such outright failures—all our futures are confined to a closed area. We have no choice but to move in intricate circles, making room for our own expansion by restricting someone else. Occasionally, some of us cannot help but find ourselves displaced. What then? There is seemingly nowhere to go.

"My firm, Mr. Sibley, meets this situation. We are

10

an old, established business. We realize that the stress of this life is particularly hard on some types of persons. This problem is even more greatly magnified in business circles, where it can bring the ordinary pressures of social competition even nearer the insuperable. And being a businessman today is often painful, isn't it, Mr. Sibley?"

Again the man nodded, and Sibley, almost perforce, nodded an instant behind him.

"So." The man tented his hands. "My firm has now made its chief specialty the alleviation of some of the crises which can arise even in the best-managed circumstances. For example, Mr. Sibley, you have only recently concluded an agreement with a Mr. Hewes, who has been made a one-tenth partner in your brokerage house. In return, Mr. Hewes brings to your firm the advantage of his position as chairman of the Federal Securities Exchange Commission."

Sibley's face paled. He stared at the man.

The man put up a quick, disclaiming hand. "Never fear, Mr. Sibley. Our discretion is of the highest order. We are, after all, on your side of the fence. That is, should anything ever happen to this delicate arrangement, we trust you will keep us in mind. You will find us efficient, discreet and equal to the task." The man smiled for the first time—a quick, fleeting, polite twitch of his mouth. No more. "And I believe that concludes my intrusion. I trust you will find it worthwhile, at some later date, should the occasion ever arise." He stood up, still in rhythm with the room's leisurely movements, said, "Good day, Mr. Sibley," in his drifting voice, and walked quietly away.

Sibley automatically put the card in his breast pocket. He sat for what seemed like a long time, the paper drooping forward in the one hand which still held it, his other hand lying limp in his lap where it had sunk down from the front of his surtout.

Now that it was too late and the man was gone, his mind teemed with objections and questions. How had Doncaster found out? Who else knew? Was Doncaster trying to blackmail him? If so, why hadn't their representative simply stated the percentage they wanted, instead of going about it this way? What about Hewes? Sibley had certainly thought the agreement and the freedom of operation it permitted were safe. Now it seemed they were not. The leak must be at Hewes's end, somewhere. Could he trust a man who could be compromised so easily?

Slowly, the panic died down by fractions, and Sibley became aware enough of his surroundings to raise the paper in front of his troubled face again and, behind it, to think over his first excited reactions.

The ultimate corporation. It wasn't a completely unreasonable thought. In a world full of piracy and shipwreck, salvage ought to be profitable. And if that was what Doncaster was, then their interests more or less were on the same side of the fence as that of their potential clients.

Sibley bit his lip. The man's logic had been strained: he had made it sound as though business were a matter of ruthless, cutthroat competition, which it most certainly was not, and that all of life, as a matter of fact, was a tense crowding-out of one person to make room for another. That was certainly as extreme a viewpoint as Sibley had ever heard. It was most definitely not his own viewpoint.

One just had to be careful, that was all.

Nevertheless Doncaster had a selling point.

He got up slowly and walked thoughtfully out of the lounge, his footsteps quiet. He nodded absently to the servitor who held the door for him, and walked down the broad marble steps to the curb where his car drew up for him. He got in silently, and his chauffeur drove him to his office without asking.

He got out of the car at the entrance to his office building and now, finally, at the sight of that stone facade and his name in gilt on the door, at the thought of all they represented, the delayed reaction triggered off.

He walked stiffly across the sidewalk, feeling as though he was being watched by everybody. He remembered the way the man had casually twisted him around his little finger, and a blush shot up to flood his cheeks. He moved through the door in self-conscious agony, and he remembered what Doncaster's man had said to him as: *Today's society is particularly hard on* some *types of persons*. He blushed again as he seemed t. remember naked contempt on that man's perpetually expressionless face.

He knew himself well enough to realize he might be unconsciously coloring the memory to twist the dagger deeper. But that merely made it worse. He knew he was perpetually fearful. He knew he had no pride. It was ridiculous to blame anything but his own weakness. In any other time, he knew, he would have been just as pitiful.

As he walked through the lobby, with its people, he seemed to see cold amusement on every hand. His arms jerked upward in an aborted reflex that would have been a gesture of self-protection. But he stopped in time, since there was nothing visible in front of him to protect himself from. His fingers did lose their hold on the newspaper, however, and he had to stoop and pick it up in the middle of the crowded lobby.

In his office he sat trembling, his nerves unstrung. There were a dozen urgent matters waiting to be attended to, and he forced himself to them. Then he lost himself in them, ticking them over in his brain like so many punched cards. In the solitude of his office, engrossed in his work, there was no hesitation in him, and a certain joy. Tonight, later, he would review his decisions again and again, wondering if he had made a mistake. But now he was decisive; sell here, buy there. This company, A, would soon have no choice but to merge with that company, B. His staff of market analysts did not have to tell him that—he could feel it as surely as a breeze on his cheek. Buy. And when they merged, their chief competitor, C, would take a severe jolt. Sell.

The world in which he moved was held as surely in his mind as the map of a familiar country. He knew it well. It compensated for much that he could be sure he knew it well. He had a mathematician's—or, better, a strategist's mind for it.

Then he shuffled farther down through the stack of papers. The manager of the Stock Exchange had to be sent his monthly consideration, or he would begin unaccountably losing track of Sibley's bids. Sibley inched his cramped signature across the bottom of the check.

His contact men in the rival brokerage houses were also due for their checks. He signed those.

There was a voucher for ten per cent of the previous day's commissions, made out to a fictitious name. That was the cash for Hewes's dummy bank account. There were other payments to be made, to other necessary people.

And once that was done, he sat looking down at the signed orders and checks, his mouth dry. In the back of his mind, something nagged him that nagged him every day after a spasm of work. He looked around the well-furnished office, and felt drained.

He was forty-nine, and he was alone. He had learned

14

his skill from his dead father, and been born to this office. He worked with numerals on paper, and his head was full of averages and balances. His accomplishments were figures in bank books, certificates in safe deposit boxes. From somewhere, a notion pulled at him that a man should leave the mark of his hands on the world; something built—something created. That came from his boyhood, probably. He remembered the intense concentration, the patient effort, and the almost boundless satisfaction of putting a toy model together. His room had been full of ships and aircraft, painstakingly shaped. He found himself remembering the turn of a keel and the flowing airfoil of an outthrust wing—

"Miss Pierson!" His fingers jammed down on an intercom stud.

"Yes, Mr. Sibley?"

"You can come and take this away now."

He sat despising himself. Was he a man or a weakling? He knew the answer but, since he knew it, was he so completely spineless that he couldn't even discipline himself? It was enough that he knew the mechanics of his work. He ought to be proud of knowing them. He was a top craftsman in his field, and his firm was successful. It made not the slightest bit of real difference whether he hated the things he had to do to insure its success. He ought not to hate them. A man—a real man—would never let his mind betray him into thinking things that were absolutely profitless. He thought too much. He tortured himself too much.

Miss Pierson came quietly through the door, and Sibley hastily rearranged his features, knowing it had been too late and Miss Pierson would be smiling slightly behind her decorous mouth.

He did not look up. She gathered the signed papers. "Will that be all, Mr. Sibley?"

"Yes—no. Put a call through to Mr. Hewes, at the Securities Exchange Commission."

"Mr. Hewes. Yes, Mr. Sibley."

Something in her voice made him suddenly realize his mistake. He couldn't call Hewes. Not from here. Panic touched him. He'd dropped his guard for a moment, and now he had to make up for it hastily, as best he might, and hope no damage had been done.

"No—wait. I'll have lunch with him and talk it over in person." He knew Miss Pierson was one of Claffin & Sharpe's contacts. There was no doubt in his mind that Hewes would have an interest in their firm, too, but he couldn't have them suspecting he was in trouble. He looked up, and caught a quick glimpse of the expression hovering around the corners of Miss Pierson's eyes. "Ah —there are some aspects of the new SEC code that I want to discuss . . ."

Miss Pierson was close to laughing at him openly, he knew. She must have realized long ago that he was aware of her double function. As long as Claffin & Sharpe didn't also know that, it would make no difference to her. But she must derive constant satisfaction from watching him try to fool her whenever there was something he didn't want her to know.

"Of course, Mr. Sibley. Shall I arrange an appointment?"

"No—no, thank you, Miss Pierson. I'll do that myself." He twisted in his chair. "Tonight. At home."

"Of course, Mr. Sibley."

She turned and walked quietly away. Sibley followed her with tortured eyes, thinking how attractive a woman she was.

He called Hewes's private number from his novel-lined study at home, his stomach uneasy. The face on his phone screen, too, seemed a little unsure of itself.

16

"Yes, Sibley?" Hewes asked in a cautious voice.

"Ah—Mr. Hewes, I'm sorry to trouble you at your home. But our firm had a call today, just at closing time, from a customer who wanted shares in a firm called Doncaster Industrial Linens."

He peered closely at the screen. Hewes would be working just as hard as he at keeping up an impression of innocence over anything as public as a phone line. But he was almost sure he could see a slight twitch in the man's eyelids.

"Yes, Mr. Sibley?" Hewes said after a moment.

"Well, we'd never heard of it." He acted out an expression of slight embarrassment, suspecting it couldn't fool anyone examining a recording of the call, but hoping he was wrong. "That seemed odd in itself. And it *was* closing time, so we couldn't check the Exchange. Now, we'd want to put the bid on the market as soon as possible tomorrow, if it's a legitimate concern. So I thought I'd call you and ask if, offhand, you could remember the firm and tell me whether it was reputable."

Hewes looked at Sibley for a meaningful second. His eyes were a little frightened, too, and yet oddly relieved.

"It's a small firm. But, I'm sure it's reputable."

Sibley hadn't been sure what he might accomplish with the call. Certainly, if anyone ever began to check back, it was a damning piece of evidence. But that would hardly matter if anyone ever began checking back. He'd had to make the call—and today, not later, or his night would have been unbearable. Now he knew that Hewes had been as upset as he was. Now a relieving thought had come to him.

Hewes confirmed it. "I happen to know of it by an odd coincidence, as a matter of fact," Hewes said with elaborate casualness. "I received an inquiry from a private investor today, myself." His hand moved toward his inside breast pocket, where his card case would be, and he looked meaningly at Sibley.

A wave of relief washed through Sibley's nervous system. Hewes *had* also been contacted then. It meant, or at least it seemed to mean—and that was the best anyone could hope for—that Doncaster was what it said it was. There were no certainties in this world, but it was at least possible to believe the agreement between Hewes and himself was not an open secret.

"That *is* odd," he said. "Well, thank you, Mr. Hewes, I'm sorry to have troubled you."

"Not at all, Mr. Sibley. I'm *very* glad you called," and Sibley realized quite plainly that Hewes had been afraid the leak came from Sibley's end—that Sibley might even have engineered it. The reverse possibility had occurred to Sibley.

"Well, good night."

"Good night."

They hung up. Sibley, alone in his empty house, sat for hours in his study. The worst fear was over. If Doncaster represented a threat, they were going about it in too complex a way to be believable. It was much more logical that they should be exactly what they claimed.

But now, by a common human paradox, he had time to think of all the things that might have happened. Behind the graphic scenes he created to torment himself—the slow sucking away of his firm's assets, or the sudden public exposure of his and Hewes's arrangements—lay the great, cold fear that rode his shoulder night and day. He pictured himself suddenly stripped of everything he and his father before him had struggled to create and maintain; the good name, the social position, the eminent standing of the firm on which both depended.

He beat down, with disgust for his own weakness, the secret voiceless yearning for just that release. He reminded himself: Where would he go? What would he do? Stripped of every human dignity and every social advantage, he could only whirl down into the gray mass of ordinary people drudging through vague lives somewhere beyond the borders of the social sphere.

He went to bed at last, his mind working in tighter and tighter circles. When the light was out and the darkness pressed close, he found himself picking again at his fear of Doncaster.

They knew so much! He could picture their contacts, infiltrating his firm, and Hewes's office, and God knew how many other places. If they were what they claimed, they would necessarily have a network rooted through every important stratum of the world, like some secret growth.

Everyone lived in the palm of everyone else's hand. Miss Pierson's employment by Claffin & Sharpe depended entirely on his pretending not to know what she was. One move on his part, and she would lose that position —and someone else in his firm would go on their payroll.

And Claffin & Sharpe's continued operation depended on his not using what he knew about them. While he, in turn, was dependent on Claffin & Sharpe's not exposing what they knew of him. And both of them, in turn, depended on and were depended upon by an interwoven host of third parties like a circle of men holding knives at each other's throats.

Even Hewes was not safe. If anything ever happened to Sibley—if some day a saving ulcer should burst through his stomach wall—the Inheritance Tax Division of the Bureau of Internal Revenue would automatically impound all his records and review all his conversations.

Everyone lived on sufferance. That was the way of the world. But now there was one more pair of eyes poised at his back.

He lay in his bed, torturing himself and desperately

wishing he had never agreed to go into this thing with Hewes. It made no difference to his wild mind that he couldn't have refused. His position on the Exchange would have been made impossible for him. But he should have thought of *something*.

He worked himself into a state of nerves, tossing exhausted among his tangled sheets and far too strung up to get the sleep he desperately wanted.

Stealthily, the revulsion with himself crept out to encompass the world he knew, and he had wild fancies of himself suddenly grown decisive and powerful, smashing down one opponent after another until all of them—Claffin & Sharpe and all the rest—were down in ruins, and only he towered over the world, and there was no one left powerful enough to threaten him. And then—and then he could let it all go, and creep away to some bit of land, somewhere, with trees and a lake, where the air was quiet and the nights were calm.

He buried his face in his hands on his pillow, shaking, knowing how far away he was from being any such colossus—how much of himself he poured out every day just to maintain his insecure position among the firmer, better men with whom he shared his world.

Toward dawn, he fell into something that was half dream and half delirium. It seemed to him that he floated above the earth on a fleecy cloud. Soft, resilient, white and pure, the cloud cradled him and lulled him in a warm sunlight far above the jagged mountains and cold oceans waiting gray and ugly below him.

There was darkness and brooding menace at the bottom of the gulf he overhung, as though some implacable appetite knew where he was and waited for him.

The cloud supported him, but he knew with all logic that no cloud could possibly support a man. He waited for whatever amnesty it was that held him up to be removed, and for his fall. Meanwhile, he ate constantly at

20

handfuls of some wonderfully palatable substance that seemed to be all about him.

It was the cloud, of course, he realized as he ate the last of it and fell.

Sibley put his hands up to his face and throat.

In the morning he arose and was driven down to his office, and each day for six years thereafter, a little more bent, a little more fearful, a little farther down the road to hell. For six years, nothing changed. He grew richer, and Hewes grew richer. The business card in his wallet turned shabby, but he never threw it away.

And then Hewes doubled over at his gymnasium, clutching his chest and choking, the squash racket spilling away from his hand. His overstrained heart tried to hold itself together, but he had punished it once too often. His opponent was a physician, and he had the best possible help almost immediately, but there is just so much that can be done. The Inheritance Tax Division took its routine steps, and Sibley was left walking around and around a building in downtown New York on a gray December afternoon.

Sibley walked on, not knowing what to do. Suddenly, when he had to use the card, he realized how little the man who gave it to him had actually said. He moved in a cloud of panic, unable to decide whether he was thinking rationally or deliberately torturing himself.

But what *had* the man said, after all? Almost nothing; a collection of generalities and implications. He might have misunderstood the whole thing.

Well, no—there was the way Hewes had acted, and the whole business of Doncaster's knowing about him and Hewes.

He turned the next corner, and the next, and was at

the front of the building once more. He turned toward the entrance, determined to go in this time.

But at the sight of the door actually in front of him, he suddenly realized that he *might* have misunderstood everything—that out of a few inconsequential threads he might have woven a whole cloth of wishful mis-impression. They would laugh at him, inside, for confronting a towel company with a sea of troubles.

An unexpected touch laid itself against his forehead, and he looked up, startled. It was snowing lightly, sifting down among the bluff buildings, blurring the hard outline of stone against sky and veiling the geometric distances of the streets.

He turned his head from side to side, uncertain, his thinking out of kilter. He knew the snow would be brief, held back as soon as the first people left their offices at the end of the business day. But meanwhile he would be increasingly uncomfortable, here outside. He should have paid attention to the weather forecasts, but there was so much to keep track of. So much . . .

He snatched a quick, surreptitious glance at the few people still on the street. But all of them were bent forward as they walked rapidly by, the mark of the snow on their clothing and in their movements. Ducking his own head, Sibley thrust himself up the steps and into the building.

He pushed through the door and found himself in a narrow hall. He looked around, trying to see into the darkness. He found the lift shaft and stepped into it, punching the number from memory. When he stopped, he got out, automatically sure that he'd picked the wrong floor, or the wrong building. He thought he'd had it right, but he doubted himself so much that he had to take the card out and check it, and only then remembered that, of course, he'd seen the name plate downstairs.

He walked slowly up the dark hallway, looking hesitantly at cheaply lettered names on dirty glass doors. He avoided the inquiring glances of the occasional receptionists who looked up from inside various officies.

At last, he came to the door labeled DONCASTER INDUS-TRIAL LINENS. He looked through the glass and saw six or seven other people waiting their turn beside the receptionist's switchboard. Some of them were very poorly dressed; others looked better-off. They sat without looking at each other, an awkwardly assorted group. The receptionist was oblivious to them, and to anyone in the hall. Unlike the other offices, Doncaster's was busy.

He pushed through the door and crossed the front office to stand waiting in front of the receptionist's desk.

"Yes?" The receptionist did not change expression. She looked up at him with obvious impatience to get back to her transcribing.

Sibley held out the graying, dog-eared business card. "I—excuse me. I have this card . . ."

"Um-hmm?"

Sibley broke. He thrust the card into her hand. His temples were hammering. "My—my name is Allen Sibley," he blurted. "I need help."

II

THE RECEPTIONIST lifted one eyebrow. She turned the card over in her hand, inspecting both sides. Her fingernail scratched at it, and a faint green tinge appeared in the paper. Then she reached out without looking and touched a button on the switchboard. Her lips moved behind a square of opacity that sprang up in the air in front of them, and there was no sound.

Sibley's eyes fastened on her face, hunting for a clue to what she was saying.

She glanced up at him frigidly. He rubbed his hand over the lower part of his face and dropped his eyes.

"Mr. Sibley."

He could see her lips once more, and she was handing back his card. "Yes?"

"Please go right in. Mr. Small will see you. You'll find him through that door; the first office on your left."

"Thank you . . ."

The receptionist was already back at work. He moved uneasily through the gate beside her, conscious that the people on the visitors' bench had raised their heads and were looking at him indignantly. He went through the door into a corridor of frosted glass doors, each with a name lettered on it. He looked to his left and saw one lettered MR. SMALL. He opened it with a tentative push.

He saw a desk, and a spare, middle-aged man with thinning hair, dressed in a dark blue soutane. The man was looking at him with a troubled expression.

"Mr. Small?"

The man came around the desk and extended a dry-skinned hand. Sibley shook it, and the man dropped his hand quickly and motioned toward a chair. "Very glad to meet you, Mr. Sibley. Sit down, please," he said in a voice tinged with embarrassment. He went back around his desk and sat down with a sigh. He looked at Sibley, and his lower lip drew in between his teeth for a moment. "Frankly, Mr. Sibley," he said, "we wish you hadn't come here."

The last of the snow was coming down now, the frequency of the flakes decreasing steadily. Sibley hunched forward in the chair and watched it dully through the office window. "You can't help me," he said in a dead voice. His face slowly lost hold of all expression, and his complexion faded down into gray.

Small shook his head quickly. "I didn't say that, Mr. Sibley."

"Oh? Well, then . . ." Sibley's head rose, and his shoulders straightened.

Small picked up a self-powered desk clock and put it down on the blotter in front of him. His fingers pushed it back and forth. "Doncaster never turns down a client, Mr. Sibley. That's our policy, and we keep to it, invariably. We have a very high reputation to maintain." He pushed the clock away. "This means we sometimes have to take on a client when we would rather not."

Sibley stared down at the floor. His arms draped forward across his thighs, and his hands dangled at the end of his wrists. He tried to think of something to say, but there was nothing. The only thing he could do was sit here at Small's mercy, and wait for him to explain. His mouth twitched. Not even Doncaster wanted him.

"Mr. Sibley, there's nothing personal in this," Small was saying. "We simply try to avoid cases as complicated as this one. You'll grant me that even in today's milieu, the examination of Mr. Hewes's records will create a scandal and investigation of unusual proportions. The federal government will have no choice but to clean house. The reputation of the entire securities exchange system is at stake. There will be a determined effort to prove that Mr. Hewes was actually the dupe of an organized conspiracy by the brokerage houses and stock companies."

Sibley's panic doubled. He felt the familiar sickening convulsion in his stomach. He hadn't thought it out that far, but now he saw Small was right. Every effort would be made to blame him far more than Hewes. He had envisioned bankruptcy and disgrace. Now he realized he might well go to prison for a very long time.

He looked at Small in despair. If Doncaster didn't help him he was totally lost. He said nothing. He simply looked at Small, and let Small see his feelings on his face.

A fleeting expression of revulsion flickered in Small's eyes. He made a sour mouth and pulled the desk clock toward him. He fastened his glance on it as he toyed with it and spoke to Sibley without looking up.

"There's no need for panic, Mr. Sibley. I mention these things only to point out that the federal government will certainly make a searching investigation—searching enough so that any falsification of records or arrangement of evidence will not suffice to extricate you. We shall have to take drastic steps." He smiled wryly. "With no prejudice toward you, Mr. Sibley, I find myself wishing heartily that our salesman had been a little less ambitious." He shrugged and said, "But that's done."

Sibley looked at him helplessly. He wished desperately that Small would either let him go or state his proposition. He wished he had the resolution to demand that much. But he could only sit and wait, while the fear gnawed at his stomach and the hope of help came and went.

"Mr. Sibley, I have a reason for this circumlocution—or this apparent circumlocution," Small said dryly. He looked up suddenly and smiled coldly. "No, I'm afraid telepathy is still far in the future, even for us. The study of psychology, however, is not. Believe me, I appreciate your feelings, and I am not here to torture you. But I am trying to persuade you to agree to the only possible measure that will save you.

"First, I assure you that every other resource is useless. To substantiate that, I can only say that our experience in these matters is such that we can see success in no other solution. Our experience is long and extensive. We would not have the reputation we enjoy, nor be able to command the service fees we do, if it were not."

"I know it's going to cost me money," Sibley said impatiently. "A large amount of money. I *know* that."

"I'm glad you do, Mr. Sibley," Small said mildly. A small light of satisfaction appeared in his eyes, and then he went on, while Sibley fretted.

"But I'm sure you'd like to know what you're paying for." He held up the desk clock.

"This is a complex mechanism. Like our society, it contains a multitude of cogs and wheels. It is crammed with parts, all turning on each other, each dependent on the other. And it fits into a case. It has form—dimensions—limits. So many parts in so much rigidly limited space.

"Suppose a part breaks. It breaks beyond repair. The watchmaker removes it, and replaces it with a new one. He cannot return the old part to its place. He cannot put it in anywhere. The clock would jam, Mr. Sibley."

Get to it! Sibley thought fiercely.

"We cannot put you back where you were, Mr. Sibley. We live in a box—a clock case. We cannot put you back in the box without weakening a dozen other cogs. We cannot endanger ourselves or our other clients. We are a widespread organization. If we take half measures in your case, we endanger every other client on our list."

Sibley writhed in his chair. He'd already agreed to pay. What more was Small trying to prime him for? What was all this chatter? Sibley looked bitterly at his weak-fingered hands. If he'd been stronger, he would have survived. A man's weakness was his own fault, whether the society was complex or primitive, ruthless or not. A man born to weakness, a man with a soft body and a cringing mind, was doomed from the start, trapped in his own prison. He was a weakling, a failure and a coward. Here he sat, begging for help. Whose fault was that? It was too easy to blame anyone but himself.

Whatever his flaws, he had always been unbendingly honest about his own contemptibility.

A flash of peevish anger yapped at Sibley's heels. He slapped his hands down on the arms of his chair. "Mr. Small, either you intend to help me or you don't." He stared at Small, shocked by his own outburst. "If you do, please begin," he mumbled in a fading voice.

Small looked at him with astonished amusement—perhaps not so astonished, at that.

Sibley felt himself wilting. He tried to jut his jaw and return Small's look with a cold stare, but just at that moment his scalp began to itch irritatingly, and he had to block his face with his forearm as he scratched it. The effect of determination was completely lost.

"Of course, Mr. Sibley," Small said. "But what I have been trying to make you understand is that even we, with our resources, have our necessary limitations. We cannot stop the investigation. We cannot put the broken part back in the clock case. We can only melt it down and forge a whole new part out of it. We cannot return you to society as yourself. Do you think you'd like to stop being Allen Sibley?"

III

THE QUESTION was put casually, and it was a moment before Sibley realized Small had actually come to the point.

But something in his mind jumped into furious and wishful life, even before he could actually think. His hands began to shake slightly. Then he looked up, hearing himself talk, somehow looking out at the world from a place six inches behind his eyes.

"Drop out of sight, you mean? Change my name and

move to another part of the world? Something like that?" His throat was dry.

Small shook his head. He smiled. "Not quite. Much more than that, Mr. Sibley. I'm afraid the federal government has investigatory methods that would easily penetrate as obvious a move as that." He sat back and looked steadily into Sibley's eyes.

"We have an active and inventive research staff. Sometimes our work requires physical or psychological apparatus which no one else seems to have been interested in developing. What bears on your case is this: we have a means of completely and genuinely changing the entire physical appearance and personality of any human being. I'm sure it can be adapted to your needs."

Sibley's glance fled through the window and locked on distance.

The snow had stopped entirely. From where he was he could see Long Island emerging from the obscurity of gray, and the broad Atlantic heaving beyond it.

"The method is quite safe, quite fast, and foolproof," Small was going on. "Personality alteration by this method consists of changing such physical determinants as the basal metabolism. With an altered rate of glandular activity, a change in nervous reaction times, and a general re-working of the body's efficiency as an organism, a marked difference inevitably occurs in one's attitude toward the world and oneself. You would be amazed at how much a minor physical weakness or a glandular imbalance can do to a man's general personality. Remove the weakness, correct the imbalance, and an entirely new and unexpected person emerges. We are amazed, frequently, at the potentialities which lurk, obstructed and obscured, clamoring for release, in the most workaday specimens of humanity." Small pursed his lips in a bemused smile. "I say we are surprised," he murmured, "and, indeed, *we* are, looking on from outside the man's consciousness. But I think even the most crippled of us all suspect the true, straight shape of themselves. I think perhaps that is what helps cripple them; they look at themselves as they are, and sense there is something wrong, somewhere—that something has robbed them outrageously. They become apprehensive; suspicious. Yes . . ." He made a sudden, sharp gesture, as though he did not like that mood.

"Very well; so much for the personality change. That by itself will go a long way to throw an investigator off the track. The physical result, as you may have guessed, follows naturally from this process and is equally impressive. Your body will be in perfect health. Not simply 'excellent,' but perfect. It will function with razor-keen efficiency in dealing with its own requirements. It will burn off excess flesh and add what is deficient. Once it has established its own perfect balance, no more than reasonable care on your part will keep it that way.

"In addition, we provide new retinal patterns and finger and toe prints ¬.ithin a few days of your leaving here, Mr. Sibley, you will be a completely different man —unrecognizable to anyone who knows you now, no matter how intimately. And within a few weeks—forgive me for saying this; it would be true of anyone—a *better* man."

Sibley did not turn toward Small. If he kept looking out the window, he could concentrate on that and forget the working of his face.

A sea bird, lost from its usual haunts, flapped purposefully downriver, too preoccupied or too tame to do more than dip and rise slightly out of the paths of equally stolid commuters who, if they noticed it at all, simply touched the MacDonnel powerpacks at their belts and altered course in turn. Like any other homeward-bound traveler, lost in thought and passing through a crowd of casual acquaintances, the bird nodded and curtsied its way out to sea.

"You will, of course," Small said, "retain your awareness of yourself, as well as your memories. We do not touch the brain. We do not have to. The human brain, given half a chance, is quite capable of looking after itself. You will find yourself essentially the same—but in a much better setting, and with a different outlook on the world.

"What do you think of that, Mr. Sibley?"

Once again, Sibley seemed to be standing behind his own eyes, seeing the other man in a spot of clear vision surrounded by hazy blackness. His heart was thudding in his chest.

"What . . ." His voice was too husky to carry through. He tried again. "What happens afterward?"

Small frowned. "Afterward? Oh—I see." He smiled. "Afterward, Mr. Sibley, you walk out of this building, with complete new identity papers. We will insert duplicates wherever necessary in the various record-keeping bureaus, and produce, when needed, witnesses who attended school with you, worked with you, lived in the same building—whatever seems necessary, in the unlikely event that your new personality also does something to attract investigation." He tented his hands. "It has been our experience that these new personalities are quite well able to handle themselves in any situation, and rarely encounter difficulties they cannot resolve themselves."

Sibley asked: "How much?"

"A quarter of a million dollars, Mr. Sibley."

The figure sucked the air out of Sibley's lungs. "You're joking. I barely have that much in my personal accounts."

"A few thousand more than that, yes. We rounded it off for convenience' sake. It will not be necessary for you to make a formal withdrawal. We'll attend to it."

Sibley looked at him bitterly. "I'll never be able to

touch any of my other assets. I lose those, too. Just what am I supposed to do with this new personality, if I'm penniless? You're offering me no choice at all."

"You have a choice, Mr. Sibley. You can leave here a new, dynamic and free man. When we make the withdrawal from your accounts, we'll pass the surplus on to you. Any number of people would consider a few thousand dollars an excellent start in life.

"Or, you can refuse the offer, keep your money, and leave this building with imminent prosecution waiting for you. If you want to, Mr. Sibley, you can stay exactly the man you are."

Sibley could not stare him down. He dropped his eyes, seeing clearly how Small had been playing with him, how surely he had twisted every weakness in him, and how much he must know of the frightened, miserable Allen Sibley.

His aching fingers unclenched. Sweat was trickling down the walls of his chest. "All right," he said.

Small nodded without surprise. He looked at Sibley the way an animal trainer looks with satisfaction at the dog jumping through the hoop.

Sibley's face burned. But soon, he knew, with a sudden joy, that would never happen again. Soon he would be a man.

IV

HE SAT in his assigned room, somewhere in the building which was as full of Doncaster offices as a corncrib was of ratholes. The operation—he had no other word for it —would be taking place soon.

He sat on the edge of his chair, with Small sitting opposite him, his mind like a clenched fist around the thought of what he'd be like tomorrow. It made no difference that Small had told him the full process wouldn't complete itself for several weeks.

Tomorrow he'd be lithe and muscular. More important, tomorrow he wouldn't be himself. No more self-torture, weighing, judging, laughing at his own pitifulness, sneering at himself. No more being alone, surrounded by nothing but enemies. Tomorrow he'd be a man. He'd be away from this endless raking-over of every move he made, every word he said. He could leave his rabbit-warren brain behind.

For the first time, he dared admit to himself that for a long time, now, he had been hating his own intelligence for the ease with which it enabled him to dissect himself.

"Perhaps we're being hasty," Small said, breaking in on him. "The government might decide to hush it up. Or perhaps we might be able to attack the problem by more conventional means, after all."

"No," Sibley said quickly. "No, the government doesn't act like that. This is the only way."

"We can't be sure. Why don't we wait? There's always time if this does prove unavoidable."

Sibley looked across the room in something near panic. "This is my last chance to get away."

"It would be foolish to go through all this procedure only to find it was unnecessary."

"Small . . ." Sibley cut himself short as he realized Small was playing with him again, deliberately prodding his panic like a muleteer with a goad.

Sibley looked down. *Enjoy it*, he thought bitterly. *Enjoy it while you can.*

Small looked at his watch. "It's time, then."

Sibley rose quickly and followed him. Tall, he was standing behind a desk, looking coldly out a window, listening while across the room stood an anxious man who looked like Small, saying: "Please, Mr. Sibley—I'll be more careful in the future. I don't know where I'll go if you don't give me a chance, this one time."

"Careful there," Small said.

Sibley realized he'd stepped on Small's heel as they turned into the hall. "Sorry," he mumbled. He followed Small down the corridor, but because he was behind the man he carried his head at a proud angle.

"Now, afterward," Small said over his shoulder, "you'll go back to your room. There'll be clothes, identification papers and money there. You'll be staying here for a few days, until the process is well advanced, and you'll need some cash to pay for meals we'll bring up to you. Tomorrow, we'll make the withdrawal at the bank, and you'll be given the surplus. You'll find facilities for making out the identification papers to any name and physical description you choose. Your new retinal patterns and fingerprints are already on them."

"All right," Sibley answered curtly.

"Good." They came to a doorway, and Small knocked. A man in a doctor's uniform opened the door and stood aside, waiting. Small turned to Sibley. "Good luck, Mr. Sibley. I won't be seeing you again. Unless, of course, you change your mind now and decide to stay in your present person?"

Sibley was peering past him into the room, where bulky medical apparatus gleamed white in the cold light. A padded table lay at the focus of two descending projectors with long, gleaming, needle-sharp tips.

He jerked his head back toward Small. Suddenly, the twist of the man's thin mouth had cut deep once too often. He burst out: "You think you know everything that makes people tick, don't you?"

Small looked at him evenly for a moment. His clerkish

34

face took on an expression Sibley had never seen on it before.

"No. But I know a great deal about myself. I find it serves as an adequate guide." He turned and walked off.

"This way, Mr. Sibley," the doctor said. Sibley followed him in. He scarcely heard Small's light footsteps fading away as he looked around the room. A headset rested on the table, trailing thick wires that led to a bank of switchboards and instrument panels.

It had to be worth it. Stubbornly, he set his teeth.

The doctor flicked a finger toward a form clipped beside an array of switches. "We've built up your personality profile very nicely, I think," he said.

Sibley nodded because he felt some such reaction was expected. He looked away.

He'd been surprised, at first, because the tests he'd undergone were not at all what he'd expected. He hadn't been asked to baldly list his specifications for himself. Instead, there had been a series of apparently random questions, none of them blunt.

He'd understood their subtlety, finally. He would have hedged; if things had been conducted in a straightforward manner, he would never have dared ask for what he wanted—provided, first, he knew exactly what that was. But, as a pattern emerging from harmless answers on a psychological test, the man he wished he was had simply appeared out of his subconscious.

So Doncaster got what it wanted, and he got what he wanted, and there was really no reason to be ashamed of looking the doctor in the eyes.

He felt a brief tingle in his upper arm, rubbed it pettishly, then looked up and saw the doctor just putting down a hypodermic pistol.

"Mild sedative," he explained. Several assistants were moving about the room, setting up apparatus and running tests on the controls. One of them touched a switch,

35

and crackling green haloes coalesced around the tips of the projectors over the operating table.

Sibley touched his lips with his tongue. He felt the sedative damping his nervous reactions, but his mind was still free to work. Surgery was correction, and correction was pain. Pain was fear. Fear was weakness. Weakness was inferiority. Inferiority required correction. And correction was—

He caught himself with a gasp.

"Will you undress, please?" the doctor said.

He hesitated painfully. Atop his fear was his shame at his body's sloppiness. But it would be worse to turn back now. He could never face Small.

Moving compulsively, he stripped off his clothes and lay on the table. He couldn't bring himself to keep his eyes open and stare up at the dipping muzzles of the projectors. He couldn't restrain a shudder when the cold metal of the headset was slipped over his skull. He lay as still as he could, waiting for the pain, dreaming of those first moments when he could look in a mirror and see himself looking steadily back.

There wasn't any pain. He felt cheated. Then he flicked up an eyebrow and chuckled at himself. He yawned. He stretched, looked up at the twin projectors and grinned. He sat up.

"Well! How long'd it take?" he asked the doctor.

"A few hours."

Sibley twitched his shoulders. Well, he thought, let's give the old boy a pat on the back. "Good job, too. Feels good. All done?"

The doctor nodded. "That's right. In the event you're wondering, the fingertips and eyes are organic, but artificial. Neither your prints nor retinal patterns have ever been registered anywhere before. The same for the pore pattern of your skin."

Skin? He looked down at a familiar birthmark, and discovered it missing. For a moment, cold panic touched his stomach with nausea.

"You have a new skin," the doctor went on. "We . . . did not think it advisable to inform you in advance of that part of the process."

Well. Well, *well!* A new skin, eh? He grinned at the doctor. "Be darned. Huh! But I guess you were right in not telling me. I don't think I'd have liked it much."

The doctor cleared his throat. "If I may say so, there already seems to have been a considerable change in your personality."

Sibley laughed. His eyesight was crystal-sharp, and his body tingled with blood that raced through his veins instead of flowing sluggishly. "D'you give me everything the profile called for?"

The doctor nodded. "You're going to be completely unrecognizable as soon as the remainder of the physiological process completes itself."

Sibley laughed again. He slid off the edge of the table, grimacing at the bulge of his stomach. "Well, I guess that's that. Thanks, Doctor."

He padded across the room and opened the door.

"Ah—" The doctor was trying to catch his attention. Sibley half turned and cocked an eyebrow at him.

The doctor was holding up his discarded pants.

"What's the matter, Doc?" Sibley inquired. "Never see a naked man before?" He shut the door behind him and went up the hall to his room.

He found his new clothes in a closet in his room, and a wallet on the desk beside a typewriter. Spread out beside it were his new identification papers.

He took a long look at himself in the closet mirror.

He looked taller, and younger. And a good deal more alive. His eyes were sparkling, and he had trouble recognizing himself. The new skin had taken the old, deep-cut lines out of his face, and his facial muscles weren't sagging any longer. He was still soft, and he was still close to fifty years old, but he didn't look it, even this soon. He stood naturally straight, with his shoulders up. It was surprising how much difference that made in the shape of his stomach.

Looking himself up and down, he whistled ribaldly, grinned at himself, and began reaching the clothes down off the closet hooks.

He grinned even more deeply, climbing into them. Small must have had a fair idea of the man who'd come out of the operation. The pantaloons were comfortably colorful, the blouse was salt white with ruffled edging, and the vest was handsomely embroidered. All of them had adjustable seams.

He frowned a little over that, but that was just Allen Sibley's social conditioning, still hanging around. Tailor-mades would have been ridiculous, considering the situation. Ready-to-wear was just the ticket for a man who wouldn't quite be the same shape on any two successive days for a while.

He looked at himself in the mirror again, and liked the look of the clothes on him. Allen Sibley, old style, would have used the word "garish."

Allen Sibley, new style, whistled between his front teeth in appreciation as he sat down to look his identification papers over.

Birth certificate. Driver's license. Driver's physical examinations record book. Social Security card. Police Registry card. Three rent receipts. Two membership cards in a pair of bottle clubs.

All of them were appropriately creased and worn. Where official signatures were required, they were signed. Where stamps were required, they were stamped.

Sibley paused for a moment, picking a name for himself. He fed the driver's license into the typewriter, thinking. Then he grinned and printed, in the space marked NAME: John L. Sullivan. He filled in AGE, HEIGHT, and WEIGHT, settling for 38, 200, and 6', 0". That was close enough to his present shape to sound more or less right, if a little idealistic. When he trained up a little, it wouldn't sound too far out of the way in the other direction. In any case, the only things that anybody ever checked seriously were the print patterns already recorded on the license.

He rummaged through the desk and found a pen and some paper. He practiced his new signature a few times, and then scribbled it loosely on the license.

Working quickly, changing typefaces as he went along, he filled in the other cards and papers to correspond. Small, he saw, had provided him with a journeyman's social security card, which was good. The idea appealed to him. He could always have it changed, if he wanted to. Meanwhile, he could work at almost anything, taking jobs and leaving them as he pleased.

He smiled to himself at the heady tang of freedom.

The treated fiber of the papers aged the new additions to match the other inscriptions. He rubbed them against the floor to finish the job. When he slipped them into the worn wallet, distributing them among the postage stamps, ticket stubs, and other odds and ends already there, he was ready to stand forth as a man with at least a suggestion of a history behind him.

He counted the money in the wallet. Fifty dollars. And a few thousand more to come. He grinned wryly.

Worth it? Damned right it was worth it! He looked at himself in the mirror. He wouldn't have traded places with Allen Sibley for any amount.

The impact of being out from under Sibley's weight was making his pulse jump in peculiar ways. He stood swaying a little, from what he guessed was reaction.

The first burst of intoxication was fading out of him, now. His grin became a smile, and he turned away from the mirror, which was reflecting him fuzzily. He walked over to the bed and sat down, almost losing his balance. He rubbed his eyes tiredly, feeling his relief at finally having got away turn into a kind of complete, relaxed fatigue he'd never experienced before.

The front of his mouth felt numb, and he mashed his lips with the palm of his hand, trying to get some feeling back into them. And then he slowly began to droop sideways, winking blearily. He lost consciousness the moment he touched the pillow.

V

THE COMPARTMENT was small and bare. Sullivan turned on his side, waking up, and looked at four walls pressing up close to him. The one beside his bunk was curved to meet the overhead, and the feeling in his stomach was the peculiar lightness of MacDonnel flight.

Something stiff was crackling in his blouse pocket, one corner digging into his ribs. He pulled out an envelope, tore it open, and took out a letter. It said:

After some deliberation, we decided that our obligation to all our clients, rather than to any one individual, made this step necessary.

There remained a little too much of an element of risk. It was conceivable that you might, in an inebriated condition, for example, or through some other such circumstance, make a slip which would endanger yourself and our organization.

One might say we were doing our utmost to fulfill our contract with you, by protecting you from your last possible danger—yourself. You may not, at present, share this view, and we regret the injury to your feelings that we may be doing you. From even a cursory glance at your personality profile, however, it becomes immediately obvious that you will find yourself quite at home on Pluto, and that, once your first heat has passed, you will see the numerous possibilities open to a man of your nature on a world less constricted than our own. At least, we trust so. Our last reports were that there was still enough of a social order remaining on the planet to enable a man to advance himself. If we are proved wrong, may we say that we feel the deepest personal regret for your inconvenience. It is somewhat difficult to maintain close contact with a world so far away from ours.

In this matter of distant communications, permit us to add the following information for your guidance:

There is no regular spaceship service between Earth and Pluto, or Pluto and Venus. Passengers are docketed as freight, and only a few of the occasional freighter spacecraft have any passenger facilities at all. Passage costs five thousand dollars.

The charge for sending personal messages from Pluto to Earth varies between five and ten dollars a word, and traffic is interrupted for periods of various length, depending on the various relative astronomical positions involved. Mail is, of course, a possibility, but it should be pointed out that letters and even word-of-mouth messages sometimes go astray.

Therefore, we seriously urge that you reconsider any hasty impulses toward communication with any legal or semi-official bodies here, bearing in mind both the uncertainty of success and the insecurity of your position should you succeed. We offer this counsel out of the deepest concern for your continued tranquility as one of our clients.

For your further information and guidance, you were shipped aboard your vessel in what was made to appear an inebriated condition brought about by undue celebration of your luck in the federal lottery. Your prize money was devoted to paying your passage to Pluto, where it is your expectation to make an excellent living on the high salaries paid skilled technicians by a group known as the Plutonian Settlers' Council. This, as we understand it, is some sort of semi-autonomous body at the head of the society extant on the planet. For the record, the friends who brought you aboard were also slightly "under the weather," and the calm judgment which might otherwise have dissuaded you from this dubious venture was therefore, regrettably, lacking.

In closing, may we offer you our sincerest good wishes for your success in your new life, and our assurances that Doncaster Industrial Linens does not frequently treat its clients so drastically. Should the opportunity ever somehow arise for us to be of further service to you, please do not hesitate to call on us.

For the Corporation, then, and for myself personally, I beg to remain,

> Your servant,
> H. Small,
> President

HS/ed

The letter was turning yellow in his hands. He dropped it and watched it turn brown, brittle, and finally black before it broke up into threads of flossy ash.

Then he got up out of his bunk and opened his compartment door. He made his way up the corridor, with the peculiar cloud-walking stride of a man under acceleration in an antigravity field. He reached a door labeled CONTROL COMPARTMENT. AUTHORIZED PERSONNEL ONLY. He opened that and stood within the doorframe, anchoring himself with his hands braced against the sides. "How far out are we?" he demanded.

There was only one man in the compartment. He was a tall, thin man with a tousled mop of brown hair. When he turned his head Sullivan could see the one day's beard on his sharp-cheeked face. His rumpled shirt was open at the neck, past the top of his underwear. He grinned at Sullivan lopsidedly. "I been waitin' for you to come out of it." He waved toward the empty flight chair beside him. "Come on in and sit down. We're far enough out so we're on automatic."

Sullivan grunted. He pulled the door shut behind him and climbed into the other chair.

"Only place there is to sit on in this clunker," the pilot said. He was looking at Sullivan with open curiosity. "My name's Ted Ingels. What's yours?"

"Sullivan," he answered in a dull voice. He looked at the field of stars on the forward screen. He'd never so much as seen an astronomical photograph before in his life. He looked out at them with a numb detachment.

"Pleased t'meet you, Sullivan. Gets lonesome, makin' this run by yourself." Ingels was peering closely at him. "You know there ain't nobody else aboard?"

"I guessed," Sullivan said. "No one ever makes this trip, do they?"

Ingels nodded. "You're the first in a awful long time. And I only make the trip when Earth's sunside of Pluto. Been ten months since my last one."

Sullivan brought the knuckles of one hand up to his mouth and unconsciously dug his teeth into them while he continued to look at the bottomless pit outside the spaceship.

Ingel's curiosity grew too much to hold. "How come

43

you're goin'?" he asked. "Not that I don't appreciate the dough. But is the Settlers' Council *really* offerin' that much?"

Sullivan shrugged. He looked woodenly at the stars and then turned away. "No chance of going back? At all?"

"Can't do it, buddy. Violate my contract, leave me wide open for penalties. Couldn't do it for any less'n ten, fifteen thousand. And that's a damn low price." For a moment, his eyes had glittered. But he shook his head. "You ain't got that much," he said firmly.

"No, I don't." Here he was, Sullivan thought. And nothing could be done about it. "Could you tell me what Pluto is like?"

Ingels raised one shoulder and let it drop. "It's all right. The biggest work got done when they turned that little moonlet into a sun. Before the development corporation pooped out. A guy like you ought to make out all right—they're cryin' for anybody that'll work. They been stranded out there a long time."

"Stranded?"

"Sure. Interplanetary Resources was this corporation. Had an idea they could mine ore, process it and ship it back to Earth, and still show a profit. Didn't sound like too crazy a idea. With MacDonnels, all you needed to do was tie a bunch of finished plates or I beams into a bundle, ease 'em up through the air, and fire 'em off toward the sun. Pick 'em up at Earth's orbit, hold 'em until Earth came around, and ease 'em down.

"So Interplanetary Resources set up this smelter, built 'em some rolling mills and a company town, and shipped a bunch of miners and mill hands out there with their families. But they cut it too fine. Ran out of capital doin' all that, and couldn't sell their stuff in enough volume. Maybe they would of made out okay, with a little more time to get set up. But they didn't. When

44

they folded up, nobody else thought it was worth tryin'. So the company town stayed out there. Nobody had passage money back, and I.R. was bankrupt, so the return passage guarantee in the miners' contracts didn't hold. They been out there a long time. Scratchin' a living the best they can. It's about like the same thing that happened on Venus. One corporation tries it and goes broke, so nobody else sees any point to repeatin' their mistake. What the hell—there's plenty of mines and petroleum fields on Earth. And the labor crews that got left behind—well, hell, they stay alive."

"Hard life, is it?"

"Hard enough, I guess." Ingels still had a few things he wanted to know. "Look—what the hell happened to you? Those buddies of yours that brought you on board —you sure they weren't dumpin' you for somebody?"

Sullivan thought over his answer. Ingels puzzled him. He had never actually met anyone like him before. Ingels' type did not move in Allen Sibley's social circles. Or, if it did, it was in some infinitely better educated, more sophisticated version. Sullivan wondered how complicated this kind of man's train of thought might be. It seemed to him quite possible that in his new social stratum, Ingels would be considered a perfectly normal specimen. He certainly spoke in the sort of syntactical pattern Sullivan vaguely understood was common among the laboring classes. But the question was, how much of him could be taken at face value? Sullivan had no way of knowing. He did know the man was waiting for an answer.

Sullivan grinned painfully. "Guess I thought it was a good idea at the time, goin' out to Pluto. Anyway, I paid for the passage. I guess it won't be too bad."

And it might not. That was the thing. He had a pretty good idea of the kind of people he'd find on Pluto. They'd be a close-knit community, strong, proud and

45

independent. The kind of a world a real man would be proud to fit into. Once he learned a trade he might be able to make a pretty comfortable living at it, and doing work he liked.

He grinned crookedly. Small *had* been right. Allen Sibley's hands had been full of money. John Sullivan's fists curled inward, as though gripping a tool.

The process that had begun on Doncaster's operating table was beginning to make itself felt. As he sat there, John Sullivan's body was undergoing enormous changes. Once-sluggish glandular secretions were suddenly pouring into his bloodstream. Nervous reactions were flickering back and forth between body and brain. His rate of breathing—the very volume of oxygen made available to his blood with each breath—the amount of oxygen supplied to his brain cells—all these were markedly different from what they had been.

Quite rapidly, on physiology's time scale, John Sullivan was leaving Allen Sibley behind. Certainly more quickly than either of them would have been capable of realizing.

Sullivan knew only that Sibley, with Sibley's ways of thinking, was drifting into the background of his personality, there to be almost totally lost.

A faint, singing delight in himself began to grow in Sullivan, surer and clearer than his first nervous elation.

Ingels seemed to have accepted his answer. The lanky man scratched at his stubble of beard. "Okay. Long's you're satisfied. Tell you truth, any time anybody does ship out with me, I'm glad to take 'em. That extra five thousand ain't somethin' I'm gonna turn down. But I always wonder."

Sullivan was only too conscious of the fact that his story would not stand up under close questioning. And he was almost positive that Ingels, given enough of a lead, could ferret his way straight back to Doncaster and from there to the Internal Revenue Bureau. Ingels represented the one man who could link John L. Sullivan and Earth, or even, in time, John L. Sullivan and Allen Sibley.

"Say!" he boomed out heartily, "How's for some food? My stomach thinks my throat's cut."

"Sure," Ingels said. "Ship'll fly herself okay. Galley's back aft. I could eat a little myself. I won't charge you but the wholesale price, either."

"Good enough," Sullivan said.

MacDonnels make a joke out of thirty-two hundred million miles. The trip out took a week, and in that week Sullivan worked religiously at getting his body into shape. He wrestled one hand against the other, one arm against one leg, every day in his compartment. He tore voraciously through Ingels' galley. He came to know what his body was capable of doing, and added that to the satisfying glow of being free at last, and of leaving softness and weakness behind him. With every flex of his arms, with each time he pulled himself up by his hands against the tension of his legs locked around a structural brace, he pulled himself farther away from Allen Sibley's world, and closer to the image in his mind of a hard-bodied, strong-minded man, ready to take his place in a society of men like himself.

Ingels lowered the ship down toward Port MacDonnel. Sullivan was in the chair beside him, looking at the screens.

"Biggest city off Earth there is," Ingels said. "Twenty thousand people. Maybe another thirty thousand on the rest of the planet. Add about twenty-five thousand on Venus, and you got it. Seventy-five thousand orphans."

Sullivan looked at the low weatherbeaten buildings, with rows of newer rectangular units lined up to one side that looked like mass housing. There were larger buildings clustered near the spacefield, some with open-throated stacks boiling industrial smoke. There seemed to be some new construction around there, too.

He looked out at the surrounding country. A jagged range of mountains marched off under a wind that tore plumes of snow from their peaks. The craggy foothills tumbled toward a foaming sea, and young forests the blue-green color of firs spread toward the horizon, broken by tilled land here and there and broader stretches of open ground that looked as though it had been farmed a few years ago and then left fallow. A roaring river burst through the mountains to the sea, and overhead the burning moon was high in the dark blue sky. Sullivan caught a glimpse of blocky gray and newer white, up among the mountains.

"MacDonnel Dam," Ingels said, jockeying the ship down. "Never finished—be *damned!* They went and finished it!"

Sullivan nodded, watching the hurried clouds scud by overhead. It looked like a good world. A good world for a man like him.

He looked downward again. "What's that other ship?" he asked.

Ingels, watching his instruments, looked up again and grunted.

"Damned if it doesn't look like Tom Allenby's. Yeah, that's what it is, all right." He grinned. "By God, I haven't seen old Tom in three years. He freights to Venus. I guess we'll have a time for ourselves tonight."

"What's he doing here?" Sullivan asked.

Ingels shrugged without taking his eyes off the controls. "It beats me. Seems to me I heard the Settlers' Council had cooked up some kind of a deal with Venus and was bringing in a lot of their people to live out here and sort of get more backs behind the wheel." He risked another look at his screens. Sullivan saw a line of people

48

coming down a ramp from the ship's side. "Yeah, guess that's it," Ingels said. "Good idea, I guess—if that's what it is. I don't pal around a lot with the Pluties. They're all right, but living out here has sort of soured them. They don't talk much."

Sullivan shrugged and went back to looking down at the world coming up to meet him. When the ship was down and Ingels snapped his switches shut, he stood up and got ready to go out. He picked up the duffel bag Doncaster had generously stowed aboard with him.

"Well, I'll be seeing you," he said to Ingels.

The man nodded. He grinned. "Say—if you're feeling lonely tonight, look in a couple of bars. Tom and me'll be in one of them somewhere. Maybe we can scare up something to do." He curved his hands through the air.

"Why—why, damn it, thanks!" Sullivan blurted, completely surprised. Having someone treat him casually as a man like himself was something he'd never known before. "I'll be there."

He climbed down the ladder onto the field, picked up his duffel bag from where he'd dropped it, and looked around. The long line of passengers off the Venus ship was filing into a wooden building close to his left. He stood watching them for a minute, and breathing in the cold, sharp air. His leg muscles tingled to the feel of a gravity just a fraction different from Earth's on the light side. He felt good. He felt alive, and on top of the world.

"Hey, bud!"

He looked over toward the voice. A man in gray coveralls was motioning to him. "Get in line!"

Sullivan didn't move. "What?"

"Go on, get in line! You gotta go through Immigration."

Sullivan shrugged. "All right," he said agreeably, and began strolling toward the building.

"*Move*, buddy!" The Immigrations clerk came closer, and gestured emphatically.

Sullivan looked at him. "Take it easy," he said. Something inside him made him want to grin joyously at the taste of anger, but he controlled it.

"Damn it, *move!*" the clerk growled. He jammed his palm against Sullivan's shoulder and pushed. "We ain't got all day to waste down here with you people."

Sullivan twitched his shoulder and his hands came up, the duffel bag thudding to the ground.

The clerk dropped his hand inside his coveralls and pulled out a gun.

Sullivan froze. He didn't know much about guns, but this looked like a picture he'd once seen of a Bofors. If he remembered the caption right, the weapon could shred him, scald him, or simply knock him down, depending on how it was set.

The clerk gestured sharply. "Get in line. You're holding up the works." He looked at Sullivan with exasperation. "You big birds always have to make trouble, don't you?"

Sullivan knew he didn't stand a chance. He picked up his bag quietly. He gave the clerk a long look, memorizing his face. Then he realized he'd probably never see him again. He laughed, turned and stepped into the line. None of the other people filing into the building had said a word. They'd stopped to watch, silently, and now they started to move, just as silently. They were pale, thin, purposeful-looking people, even the women and children. They opened the line long enough to let Sullivan step in, and then he moved forward with them, his maroon pants and vest conspicuous among the pastels of the Venusians.

Sullivan grinned to himself. So now he was one of those big birds who were always making trouble, was he? He began to whistle a tune through his teeth.

The whistle died as he stepped through the receiving door of the Immigrations shed and a clerk stamped his forehead with his basic number. He half-turned, and felt somebody fumbling with his duffel bag. He looked down. Half a claim-check dangled from the strap. Someone thrust the stub into his hand.

"Move up, *move* up," somebody mumbled with mechanical impatience. "We gotta get this nonsense over with and back to our jobs *today*." He was nudged forward, the bag out of his hand. Nobody stayed near him long enough for him to put up a protest. He was hemmed in between two pipe rails, and there were people being processed forward behind him.

"Polio, tuberculosis, VD, cancer."

Four shots blasted into his skin. Four numbers were added to his brow.

"Move up."

"Look, my name's John L. Sullivan. Who do I—"

"Pleased to meetcha. Mine's Leontovitch. Straight ahead, Sullivan. *Move!*" He was shunted forward to the next station.

"Where's your T number?"

"T number?"

"Your Tomson index, bud. Oh, *Judas*, you missed it! Squeeze back there. Well, *go on!* Don't hold up the line."

He got back to the Tomson station.

"Stick out your arm," the technician mumbled as he'd been mumbling every thirty seconds for the past twenty minutes.

Sullivan thrust his arm out and grabbed the technician's shirtfront. "Look, bud," he rasped, "what's the idea of all this? Who's in charge here?"

The technician frowned in annoyance. "This is routine." He reached up and jammed a testing needle into Sullivan's arm. He read its dial, selected a stamp from the tray in front of him, and rammed it against Sullivan's forehead. "The Plutonian Settlers' Council runs it. Your resistance to cold is above average. Now beat it."

Sullivan let go of his shirt. He shouldered his way back up the line. The people off the Venus ship were letting the hell-for-leather pace of the processing cow them, or they were used to the idea. But he wasn't, and he wasn't going to let it go on.

He got back to his old place in line. The man who'd stopped him the first time now let him go by. Apparently, he was a checker against slip-ups. Which meant that the last step in the processing was right about . . . here.

He swung toward the last clerk. "You—I want to talk to you!"

"So do I," said the clerk. "You're off the Earth ship, aren't you?" He looked down at Sullivan's red pants. "Let's see your social security card."

"What the hell's the idea of all this rush?"

The clerk sighed. "Gimme your card. What makes you think you're entitled to question our laws? You're not a citizen. If you don't like it, nobody's keeping you here."

Sullivan took a deep breath.

Then he blew it out. The clerk was right. Just because his mental picture of the world had included easy informality didn't mean the world had to revamp itself to suit. He held out his card.

"That's better," the clerk said. He grimaced down at the number. "Unspecialized journeyman, huh? Well, what's your experience?"

Sullivan shook his head. "None in particular. I want to look around for a while—pick my spot."

"How much money you got?"

"Twenty, twenty-five dollars."

The clerk looked at him disgustedly. "Restaurant meal costs fifteen dollars without a work team card. Hotel bed and shower's fifty, for one night. We don't go for bug-offs around here. Now—what's your experience?"

Sullivan shook his head. "Like I said—nothing in partic-ular. I've been taking it easy."

The clerk grunted. "Stick out your hands; palms *up*, damn it—I don't care if your nails're clean." He looked down at the raw blisters which were as near to calluses as Sullivan had got. He shook his head. "Boy! Well, there's only one place for you." He flipped a blue card at Sullivan. "Put your right and left thumbs over those squares, there. Lean forward."

Red light exploded in Sullivan's eyes as his retinal photographs were taken. He heard his card clattering through the clerk's pocket typewriter. A stamp found room on his forehead. When his vision cleared, the clerk was pushing the card into his fingers. "Here. Go through Gate E. Report to the sergeant outside."

"Sergeant?"

"Yeah, sergeant. Army's the only place for you. On your way, soldier."

VI

SULLIVAN SHOWED the blue card to the sergeant, who was a thin brown-haired man leaning against the wall of the Immigrations shed. He looked at the card, looked at Sullivan, grunted and returned the card.

"Sit," he said. "Or stand. Suit yourself. We're here until they finish processing this batch. I usually pick up two or three every time. My name's Hungerford. Any questions? They'll be answered later. Any experience? Don't make me laugh."

He leaned against the building again, and withdrew into an inscrutable brooding, his brown eyes pointed vaguely at the ground. At intervals, Sullivan heard his tongue sucking a cavity in a back tooth.

Sullivan squatted down, his back against the shed wall, and thought things over.

Next time he wouldn't let them catch him off balance. They'd pressured him through that receiving routine like a dose of salts. With room to swing, next time might be a different story.

Well . . . No. No, they were right. He should have thought of it before, but a world that had to count every penny and every erg just had to have a tight organization to make sure nothing was wasted.

But . . . Yes, *but!* He'd expected to find a world clinging by its fingertips. This was a little more like a bulldog. These people weren't discouraged, and they weren't desperate. They were too busy to stop and feel anything. Now, what the devil could Pluto possibly be busy *at?*

And what about this "citizen" business? He tried to review what he knew of the politics involved, and found it childishly simple because his information was childishly inadequate.

Pluto was still a protectorate of the terrestrial federal government, he supposed. He doubted very much if Congress had even considered any bills with regard to the colonies during the past fifty years. A man was well-informed if he so much as remembered there were still people out here. No, the old status ought to still be holding good.

All right, so Pluto was still a protectorate of the federal government; whatever that might mean. Federal couldn't hope to enforce much of anything, at this distance. It certainly couldn't be bothered trying.

So Pluto was pre-empting sovereignty. All right, so who'd care? Who could possibly get upset about it? And Pluto was organized. Well, that made sense, obviously. "Work" was the watchword. Work or fight. Be useful.

Hungerford pushed himself away from the wall, turned his head to look in a window, and grunted. "Guess they're all through for this trip. Means you're my only prize this time."

Sullivan stood up. You're in the army now, bud. All right, he was in the army. It probably wasn't a lifetime job. Given a little time to look around—*and* pick up a valuable skill or two—he could plan his next step. Meanwhile, why not?

"Got any luggage?" Hungerford asked.

Sullivan fingered the claim-check in his pocket. The duffel bag contained a spare shirt, a change of underwear and socks, a razor and toothbrush.

"Do I get stuff issued to me right away? Clothes?"

Hungerford nodded.

Sullivan pulled the claim check out of his pocket and let it fall to the ground. "No luggage."

Hungerford looked at him a little less disgustedly. "Okay, Recruit Squad, fall in," he said. "Have a smoke?"

"Thanks." Sullivan took the sergeant's light, and they walked along together, passing between the buildings of the spacefield area until they reached a parking lot. Hungerford turned toward a small truck.

"I hear MacDonnel belts have become a big thing on Earth," he commented.

"That's right."

"Good idea. I can see why it caught on—privacy, convenience. We don't use 'em here. Weather's still too unstable." He made a peculiar noise reminiscent of spitting, but didn't spit. "There's a lot of things we don't have. Most of us follow the usual human pattern. We put in a lot of time praising what we have as 'manly'—the good, old-fashioned way of doing things. Belts and weather control are decadent; effeminate; sissy stuff. Well, I suppose it makes us feel better, but we all know damned well we'd give our eye teeth for one good shipload of old-fashioned luxuries. Especially me. No fluorides in the water, and we're short on dentists."

Sullivan looked at Hungerford in astonishment. The sergeant was still the same gangling character, his hair unkempt and his manner sloppy. But he was a lot deeper than he looked.

"It used to be a lot worse," Hungerford went on. "One day Pluto and Venus were going, booming concerns. The next day they were cut off and ignored. Nobody helped us, and nobody even cared if we lived or died. We've had two generations of sitting out on a pair of dead-end streets. We didn't like it, and we don't like it. Some of us have worked around to the point where we hate a Mole.

"So I'll give you some advice, Sullivan; keep your eyes open and your mouth shut. Get out of that fancy-dress and throw it away. Don't talk about Earth. The quicker you get to be a native-born Plutonian like the rest of us, the better things'll be for you."

Sullivan nodded. He climbed into the truck with Hungerford, strapped himself in and, when the sergeant motioned, helped him close the stiff, manually operated canopy.

"Utilitarian," Hungerford grunted as he forced the canopy to fit and threw the latch. "More important uses for auxiliary power units. But when you're driving one of these things by yourself, and a rain comes up, you do a lot of cursing before you dry out again." He energized his MacDonnels, gave the wheel a nudge with the heel of his palm, and lifted the truck neatly between the roof of a shed and a light-tower.

"What about you, Sullivan? What's your excuse for being here?"

Sullivan took a last puff on the cigarette, dropped it on the floorboards and ground it out.

"Sorry." Hungerford shrugged. "I always ask. I don't

always expect answers. You'd be surprised what even a Venusian will go through before he comes out here. Or, anyway, that's how it used to be, up until a while ago. I've noticed that people come out here for some pretty peculiar reasons." He pushed down his side window and spat. "Anybody who comes out here comes out for a peculiar reason, whether he knows it or not." He jerked the window shut.

"How's Earth? Still wrapped up in itself?"

Sullivan shrugged, and let Hungerford draw his own conclusions, whatever they might be.

Hungerford pursed his lips. "Not giving anything away, are you?" he said with a sour grin. He pointed the truck down. "There we are." He waved at the army installation. Sullivan saw a field clustered with atmospheric jets. As he watched, a training group ran out to them, jumped in, and was airborne, fountaining up past the truck and dwindling into the sky. The truck rocked in their wash.

Looking farther, he saw an artillery range, and a proving ground where gun carriers and tanks were screening an infantry advance. He heard the tanks' engines growling as the truck sank down.

He looked at Hungerford. "When the man said army, I didn't know he meant an *army.*"

Hungerford sucked his tooth.

VII

"This is the day room," Hungerford said, leading him through it. He opened a door. "Barracks chief's office. Sign in, sign out, request sick call, request passes or leaves here. No passes the first two months. I'm barracks chief."

He motioned Sullivan into the room, switched on the overhead light, and went behind the wooden desk. Sullivan looked around. There was a print of Feurmann's "The Nature of Man" on the wall opposite the desk. The flare of the atomic rockets of Feurmann's time was the exact tint and shape, in miniature, of the alien sun at which the spaceship's prow was pointed.

Hungerford pulled a printed form out of the desk drawer, stabbed his finger at a line. "Sign here."

Sullivan glanced over the form. It was drawn up like a contract. He caught a glimpse of several phrases: ". . . enlist for a period of not less than five years . . ." ". . . am subject to the complete authority of the Plutonian Settlers' Council . . ." ". . . agree that three-fourths of my pay shall be in the form of lands, title conferable upon my discharge, cumulative payments to be held in escrow until such time . . ."

"Just sign it, Sullivan. What other plans do you have?" He pushed a pen across the desk.

Sullivan looked at him, and nodded slowly. He scribbled his name.

"Okay." Hungerford dropped the form in his drawer and spun the combination knob. "Come on."

He led Sullivan into the barracks proper. Rows of double-decker bunks were set down its length. A double locker stood between each pair of bunks and the next. Hungerford fumbled in his pocket and handed Sullivan a key. "Down here." He led him to a bunk. "This is yours." He tapped one of the two doors on the adjoining locker. "Your equipment's in there.

"You get three uniforms: fatigue, battle and dress. Your uniforms and equipment are numbered. You'll find the same number on your bunk, your locker and your key. Your equipment—your helmet and intercom, your armor, your mess kit, your canteen—are all in there. Each item of equipment is stamped with the amount you'll be charged if you damage or lose it. Speaking of stamps, wash your face. Latrine's down at that end. Remember what I said about your civvies. Okay, you're on your own until Reveille. You're in the third platoon of B Company. Spend your time familiarizing yourself with your gear. When your bunkmate comes in, he'll tell you how to take care of it. He'll give you the word on the routine around here. My name is Sergeant Hungerford and all statements addressed to me will have my rank appended as a form of respect for discipline."

He flung up his fist, caught Sullivan just above the point of his jaw, and knocked him down.

Sullivan raised his head uncertainly.

"I earn my respect. Don't kid yourself, Sullivan."

"Yes, sergeant."

Hungerford grinned. "I always clout the recruits. Nothing personal. If I didn't look so much like a bag of bones, I wouldn't. I don't like doing it."

Hungerford turned and walked off, shutting the barracks door behind him.

Sullivan got to his feet, rubbing his jaw. He realized he should be angry at Hungerford. Instead, he was grinning again.

He touched the locker door with the key, found his fatigues, a towel and a bar of soap, and went out to the latrine.

He threw his civilian clothes into a wastecan, took a shower and dressed in his fatigues. He worked with their seams until they fit, then stood in front of the mirror the men used to check their gear before inspections.

The man who looked back at him certainly wasn't even Allen Sibley's third cousin. He wasn't quite John L. Sullivan, either. Not the Sullivan he intended to become, at least. There hadn't yet been time enough for that. But his cheeks were flatter and his eyes less puffy than Sibley's had been. His stomach was still soft, though it wasn't suety. The hardness would be in those muscles soon. Sullivan shrugged. Not at all bad for a week's time.

He used the latrine barber which, since it had no settings, presumably delivered the regulation haircut. The scalplock cut felt a little strange, but it felt good. He'd had no idea a skull wasn't shaped in one smooth curve.

Looking at himself in the mirror, he thought: Well, bud, you're in the Army for sure now, ain't you?

Yeah, I guess I am. For a period of not less than five years. But I get my lands, title conferable upon my discharge.

He wondered how much the pay amounted to, and whether, in this peculiar army, he *would* pick up some skills that would be useful on the outside.

A lot of things had happened to him today. He wondered how it would all work out—whether he'd fallen into something good, all things considered, or whether he was going to wind up in trouble up to his neck. Gathering up his stuff, he walked back into the barracks. He stowed the soap and towels and stood looking at his equipment.

He took his helmet down and dropped it over his head, fiddling with the earpieces until they felt just right. Foam padding took the shape of his head and held it. He raised and lowered the visor experimentally. It had transparency settings, turning darker or lighter at a touch. There was a setting marked UV, and another beside it, marked IFR. He tried those, and discovered the helmet light could throw either ultraviolet or infra-red, as well as a regular beam, and that with the visor he'd be able to see in the dark by either means.

He picked up his intercom collar, dropped it over his shoulders and connected it to his helmet. He kept

60

away from the switches. The whole rig was beautifully simple, actually, and easy to puzzle out.

He put the equipment back in his locker and sat down thoughtfully on his bunk. This was better stuff than anything he'd ever heard of. He could have sworn there was nothing like it. His native terrestrial conservatism made him react a little uneasily to all this futuristic gadgetry, but he recognized its efficiency.

And every piece was stamped: "Made on Pluto."

It looked as if, out here on the border—on this abandoned junk heap nobody on Earth paid any attention to—the settlers were building up a real government and a high-powered technology.

The barracks door slammed open and a wave of men came pouring in, ripping off their helmets and tossing them on their bunks, dropping packs on the floor, banging lockers and streaming toward the latrine.

Sullivan got to his feet and waited for them to see him. His glance moved among them, trying to size up each man as an individual. He didn't mind the idea of suddenly living in the same room with so many other people, but his experience didn't include anything like it. There'd be unwritten rules he'd be expected to know as a matter of course. He didn't know them. He'd have to watch the men and see how they acted; what they did in a given situation.

"Hey! Hey, here's a new one!"

He'd been spotted by a little wiry man. All the faces turned in Sullivan's direction. He stayed where he was. The best thing to do was to stay put and let them look him over.

The little man came toward him with short, quick steps. He looked up at Sullivan. "You don't look like no Venusian."

Sullivan looked down at him. "I ain't from Venus."

There was a slight noise among the other men. The little man grinned broadly. "Well, I'll be damned. When'd you get here, Mole?"

Sullivan narrowed his eyes. "This afternoon. My name's Sullivan. John L. Sullivan." He stuck his hand out slowly and deliberately. There was a faint singing in his ears.

The little man ignored his hand. He grinned nastily. "Maybe I'm jumpin' the gun?" he asked. "Maybe you're just from some other part of Pluto we don't know about. That it, Mac?"

Sullivan dropped his hand to his side and looked around. Nobody in the barracks was making a move or a sound. He felt something bubbling up through his bloodstream, and it felt vaguely good.

All right, he'd listened to Hungerford's advice. It wasn't going to do him any good, with this bird.

"I'm from Earth," he said harshly.

The little man shook his head in perplexity. "That's funny," he said. "All the rest of us are Plutonians. You sure you're in the right barracks? Hey, Craddock—ain't that your locker he's foolin' with?"

Craddock was a beefy, flat-faced man with scarred lips and vague eyes. He blinked several times. "Hul? Oh, sure. Hey, you, Mole, quit foolin' with my locker. That's my locker."

Sullivan grinned, and the tips of his teeth touched each other lightly. His shoulders dropped, and his hands opened. "The hell it is, buster," he said cheerfully.

He didn't know exactly what was happening to him, inside. His arms and legs felt light. But this was John L. Sullivan's moment; this was what he'd lived for.

The little man caught the look in his eye. He jumped out of the way. "Craddock!"

Craddock got his slow feet untracked. He shuffled forward.

Sullivan was moving a lot faster. He charged in, his

62

right fist lashing out. His muscles felt as though they were crackling with electricity.

Craddock stepped inside his swing and slammed a left into his soft stomach. Craddock's heavy right fist caught his neck below the ear. Craddock kneed him in the ribs as he fell away.

"Ya miserable patsy!" Craddock grunted. "Where'd ya learn to fight?"

Sullivan gasped for breath on the barracks floor. He coughed chokingly.

He got his lower lip between his teeth and pushed himself up to his knees, shocked and so badly frightened that he began to shake violently. Craddock kicked him in the chest and he fell backward, his eyesight going dim. He tried to get up, but Craddock slammed a boot down on the back of his neck.

Sullivan convulsed like a dying animal. He hadn't ever imagined there was this kind of brutality in the world. He saw, with a burst of pure intuition, that Craddock could kick him into a sodden bag of bones and no one would intervene. The other men in the barracks hadn't made a move. That was the way it was. Nobody had any respect for a man who couldn't take care of himself, and they wouldn't help a man they didn't have any respect for.

Sullivan choked a breath and rolled over. He was aware of Craddock, standing back a little, waiting for him to get up and make his next clumsy rush so he could finish the job.

"Come on, Mole—I got more for ya," Craddock growled. The little man who, Sullivan now saw with insane perception, had Corporal's stripes on his sleeves, was standing to one side and bouncing on the balls of his feet.

"Go on, baby," the little man yelled to Craddock in a high voice. "Go on, teach'm!"

Sullivan felt a blinding explosion of hatred go through him as he looked up at the little man. His mouth opened, and he snarled. No! No, by God, he wasn't going to end here, as though he hadn't ever changed. He wasn't going to let some little rat walk all over him.

He threw himself upward, his legs driving under him. He lurched sideways, clutching at the little man standing there. He got one hand on the little man's belt and another on his shirt collar. Swinging him awkwardly, like a length of log, he swung on Craddock and smashed him in the face with the little man's skull. He lost his grip at the same time, and Craddock and the little man fell to the floor, tangling in each other.

Sullivan kicked them indiscriminately. He grabbed one of Craddock's forearms and broke it over his knee. He got his hand in the little man's hair, held his head rigid, and crushed his nose with the heel of his palm.

Then the rest of the men were swarming over him, pinning his shoulders and tripping him up. He tried to get his arms free, but there was too much weight on them. Then somebody was slapping his face. "Easy! *Easy*, you!" the man was yelling. "Come on! Snap out of it! You wanna get hung for murder?"

He shook his head in a blur, feeling the pain Craddock had put in his neck. And some of his ribs were broken.

They slapped his face again. "Come on, killer! Come on, bud. It's all over. You licked 'em. Snap out of it. Judas!" the man who was slapping him mumbled, "Get a load of the look on his face!"

Slowly, he got it through his head. "Okay," he grunted. His eyes focused. "I'm through."

The man in front of him nodded. "He looks all right now. Let him go, boys."

Sullivan found his footing. He was swaying, but he was on his feet. He wiped his hand over his face, smearing the blood where his teeth had been knocked into his lip. He looked down at Craddock and the little man. Both of them were unconscious, though Craddock was moaning.

He'd never in his life before stood looking down at a man he'd felled. His bloodstream was pulsing with the news.

The man who'd been slapping him followed his glance. He shook his head and smiled tight-lipped. "Craddock and Jones. That was some pair, as long as it lasted. T.S. My name's Goodwin. I didn't catch yours."

"John L. Sullivan," he said. He bunched his arms, almost enjoying the pain in his chest as he felt the muscles tense across his back. John L. Sullivan Nobody's patsy. A man who'd proved himself. A man who'd passed the test.

He gave Goodwin a long, hard look. He turned his head slowly and looked at the other men. They were standing in a huddle, with thin, cold grins growing on their faces as Craddock pawed feebly at his broken arm and moaned.

"My name's John L. Sullivan," he repeated in a growl. He bunched Goodwin's shirt front in his fist. "That's my locker and my bunk."

The look on Goodwin's face changed. The slightly awed smile dropped away, and a peculiar wariness came into it. "Sure," he said in a flat voice. "Nobody's arguing."

Hungerford wrapped a strip of adhesive around Sullivan's rib cage and grunted. Sullivan could smell the whiskey on his breath. The little office was full of it.

"Surprised me. I expected 'em to drag you in here." He tore another strip of tape off the roll with a savage sound. "You know you came as near to killing those two as makes no difference? Jones is going to have to get his sinuses rebuilt, and Craddock's got a staved-in head. Don't you know when to stop?"

Sullivan looked at him. He couldn't understand what Hungerford was getting at. All he'd done was protect himself. He felt a flash of anger at Hungerford's attitude.

Hungerford's eyes narrowed. He looked sharply at Sullivan. "Maybe you don't, at that." He grunted again. "Look—Sullivan, I don't think you know it, but you're in a spot to make a perfect damned fool of yourself."

"I can take care of myself, sergeant."

"Sure. And you're going to get better at it. But don't get in any more fights."

"I didn't pick this one," Sullivan said angrily. He had no intention of starting anything. He didn't have to. The other men respected him, now, and in a few days he'd be firmly established as one of them. He resented Hungerford's telling him not to do something he didn't intend to. "What happens to me if I do?"

Hungerford's mouth twitched lopsidedly. "In this army? It's taken as a sign of the proper spirit. Nobody's going to stop you officially, short of murder. And you'll probably come out on top, physically. But—do yourself a favor. Cut it short right here. We've got enough boys like you in this army already."

Sullivan growled. "Suppose somebody else tries this Mole business on me? Which cheek am I supposed to turn?"

Hungerford silently pulled a bottle out of his hip pocket and set it down on the table beside him. His expression was unreadable, but his voice, after he put the last bit of tape on Sullivan's chest, was metallic.

"Nobody's going to call you a Mole again. You can quit worrying about that. You've established an independent reputation of your own." He sighed. "You can take the wrappings off tomorrow. The stuff I gave you to chew was Vitacalk. It heals bone breaks in twelve hours. Remember the name." He turned to the bottle, unscrewed the top and took a long swallow. He looked at Sullivan for a long minute. "Welcome to Pluto."

VIII

REVEILLE. The loudspeakers in the barracks came to roaring life, and the bellow of the bull-horn turned Sullivan over in his bunk.

"All right, now, all you men on your feet! Hit the showers! Twenty minutes to Roster Formation." The speaker clicked off.

Sullivan rubbed his face. He swung his legs over the side of the bunk and dropped down to the floor, just missing Liencer, the man from the bunk below. He grunted when he hit, feeling his muscles jump with stiff pain where Craddock had clubbed him. He felt his ribs and grimaced. Hungerford had said twelve hours. It was still a good bit short of that time.

He reached under his pillow and got his locker key, and took his soap and towel out of the locker. By the time he'd done that, the other men were already in the latrine. He shuffled toward it between the tumbled bunks, still numb with sleep, his eyes unfocused in the gray light of the cold Plutonian morning.

The latrine was crowded with men scrubbing their teeth at the sinks and soaping themselves under the showers. He looked around for a vacant spot and finally found a small one. He moved into it, leaving his towel on a radiator, and began washing. The cold water streamed against his neck and back, and he slowly came awake.

He noticed he was being given plenty of room, and

grinned a little to himself, happy. Last night had made them respect him, all right. Now all he had to do was buckle down and turn into a good soldier as quick as he could, and he'd really be one of them. He had to work on that; really work on it—drive himself, if he had to. He was a new recruit—in more ways than one—and he had a lot of brand new things to absorb. He was in a completely new kind of life. He couldn't expect anybody to make allowances for him on that account. The idea was to stick right with his own business and learn it better than the rest of them, so they'd really like him.

He looked around at the other men. This was the first chance he'd really got to see what he had for barracks mates. As he moved out from under the shower, dried himself off, and waited in line to use the barber, he managed to get a fair idea.

He frowned a little. If this was typical of what the Plutonian army had, its equipment was a lot better than its men. For the first time since he'd rolled out from under Doncaster's machines, he saw men in physical shape as bad as he'd been. Only a few of the men moving quickly out of the latrine and back to their lockers were tanned and in good shape. Even they were an odd assortment of types and sizes, as though the army didn't have any physical standards at all. And the rest of them were either flabby or skinny to a painful degree. There were more men in front of mirrors, adjusting glasses, than you'd expect in this kind of outfit.

He got his shave, went back to his locker and got into his fatigues as quickly as he could, still trying to puzzle it out. Some of the other men were already moving out the door to the company street, dressed and with their bunks made up. But there was a fair handful of others just straggling out of the latrine, and some of them looked pretty awkward at this soldiering business.

68

Turning around to get his boots, he bumped into Liencer and muttered "Sorry," still preoccupied.

"That's all right," Liencer said quickly. Sullivan gave him a curious look.

"Hell, I ain't goin' to bite you, Liencer." He was in a good mood. Seeing he wasn't the only dub in the barracks had made him feel better.

Liencer, a thinnish blond man with a nervous face, said "Sure, Sullivan," uneasily. Then he smiled suddenly in response to Sullivan's grin. "Uh-look, you better get that bunk made up. Want me to help you?"

Sullivan looked around at the made-up bunks, where the blankets were stretched drumhead-tight. Those would belong to the men who knew their business. Some of the ones being made up now were pretty sloppy, but he ought to do better than that.

"All right," he said.

Liencer smiled broadly. "It's a pleasure." He went around to the opposite side. "These top-deckers look tough, but they're easy. You got room to work in, see?" He pulled the mattress cover tight and yanked the blanket up. Sullivan tried to help him from his side, but Liencer grinned again. "I guess you better let me show you, for now. Just stand back and let ol' Flash Liencer do it." his hands moved over the blankets, straightening and tucking. "See? Nothin' to it, when you know how."

He grinned again when he finished. "And there y'are! Got a quarter? Betcha it'd bounce."

Sullivan looked at the perfectly made-up bunk and nodded in appreciation. "That's pretty good. Thanks a lot."

"Don't mention it." Liencer scooped up his fatigue hat and handed Sullivan his. "Gotta get out on the street and form up for roster, now."

"Right." Sullivan walked out from beside the bunk

69

and followed Liencer up the barracks aisle. He couldn't help noticing that Leincer hadn't made up his own bunk with the same precision, and he didn't quite know what to make of it.

Out on the company street, he asked Liencer, "What now?"

Some of the men were standing in ranks. Others were leaning against the side of the barracks. Again, it was the harder-looking men; the ones who'd got out of the barracks first, who were in ranks. It was the awkward ones who seemed to be bewildered.

Liencer winked when he saw Sullivan looking at the awkward ones, and jerked his thumb toward his chest. "Stick with me, Sullivan. These birds think just because Jonesey's in the hospital the rules got changed this morning. You and me're gonna be in ranks when Hungerford and Kovacs come out. Now look, you go stand next to Saddler, over there—the one with the ears. I gotta get down with the L's. Do what everybody else does when Kovacs comes out, and you'll be O.K. I'll see you at chow. Right?"

"O.K." Sullivan nodded.

Liencer grinned and tapped Sullivan on the arm with his fist. "Right." He trotted into ranks with a backward wave of two fingers.

Sullivan walked over beside Saddler and took his place next to him. Saddler, who had a lined, windburned face and flat, china-blue eyes, turned his head, looked at him, and said nothing. He shuffled a little to one side and gave Sullivan room. Sullivan looked at him for a minute, shrugged and looked straight ahead, wondering about Liencer.

He was a funny sort of guy. He'd started out being scared, and now he was being chummy. Sullivan ran a hand over his upper arm and frowned. He'd never known anybody that reacted that way.

The gaps in the ranks were filling up quickly now. Even the men who'd been standing around were now moving uncertainly into their places. One of them stepped up on Saddler's other side. Saddler looked at him, grunted and didn't move. The other man—a pale, gangling man with his eyes glassy from contact lenses—looked at Saddler and gave ground.

Sullivan chewed his lower lip. But Liencer was a good man to have for a friend, because he obviously knew his way around. And then, Sullivan'd never had a friend before. He was grateful for Liencer's help. He decided to let it go. There were a lot of new things he'd have to get used to.

There were other barracks up and down the street. Sullivan saw there were men formed up in front of each of them, each formation with its corporal standing in front of it. Sullivan caught the curious looks some of the men in the other formations were throwing at his platoon.

He saw the door open on the barracks opposite, and a sergeant coming out with an officer behind him. Then he heard his own barracks door, and two sets of feet on the steps, and someone in the first rank yelled "Attention!" Sullivan noticed it was one of the more soldierly-looking men. He snapped into an imitation of Saddler's stance and waited.

Hungerford, holding a roster sheet in his hand, came around to stand facing the men. There was an officer with him, and Sullivan guessed that would be Kovacs. He was a lean whippet of a man, with thin, pale lips and hellfire eyes, and he raked the platoon with his glance before nodding to Hungerford.

Hungerford looked tired, but otherwise his drinking didn't seem to be bothering him much this morning. He looked over the ranks. "Goodwin. Front and center," he said in a flat voice.

Goodwin stepped out of ranks, saluted Kovacs, and turned to Hungerford.

"Goodwin, you're acting corporal. Read the roster."

"Yes, sergeant." Goodwin took the roster, saluted the lieutenant again, and began reading names. "Adams. Andrews. Brickett . . ."

There was a "Here!" in echo to each name. Goodwin didn't call Craddock or Jones. Saddler grunted softly at each omission. When Goodwin called "Sullivan!" Sullivan answered "Here!" with the same snap Saddler had given it, and a lot of the other men hadn't. Saddler grunted again.

Goodwin finished calling the roster. He handed it back to Hungerford. "All men present," he said, saluted Kovacs and went to the corporal's position at the left of the front rank.

Kovacs stepped forward. He bunched his shoulders as though he was going to hit each man personally.

"All right. Today we are going to continue trying to turn you men into soldiers. We all know most of you are a bunch of crumbs and castoffs. We all know most of you are the absolute nadir in soldier material."

He flicked up a forefinger in a scolding gesture that took Sullivan by surprise.

"However, boys, this is why you are here. Because you are here to be separated from the men. You will note the absence from today's roster of two of your brightest adornments. You will remember that those two sorry birds are now in a labor battalion, their inability to be even the worst kind of soldier having been demonstrated. This is a pragmatic army, my friends. We have no pity for you. Nobody has any pity for you. Those of you who cannot protect themselves—from anything— will be ground underfoot." He clenched his bared teeth and twisted his heel into the dirt. "—like so much offal. I ask you to bear that in mind. Sergeant, take over."

Hungerford took one step sideward as Kovacs stepped back, and thrust the folded roster into his hip pocket.

"Today, we're going through combat familiarization again. You will all draw rifles and sidearms after chow. You will be issued live grenades at the training field. Automatic weapons men will draw four clips of .25's per rifle, two belts of 20 mm's per cannon. You will all wear fatigue uniforms with battle equipment. The first man caught with his battle armor on under his fatigues will be flogged. The second man will be shot.

"Barracks inspection showed the following men failing to pass bunk orderliness requirements:" He read off a list of six names. "These men will not go to chow. They will straighten their bunks with their hands tied behind their backs, and will then fall in and stand at attention in the company street until the platoon returns from chow. Their bunks will then be re-inspected. Liencer, you just made it by a whisker again. Maybe I ought to make that seven names for punishment. Or will you be straightened out tomorrow? Let's hope so. All right, all men not on punishment will fall out at the command and go to chow. It is now 0430. You will be back from chow and fall in for weapons and equipment inspection at 0500. Dismissed."

The platoon broke up, the men trotting off without looking at the six men left behind. One of them, Sullivan noticed, was the man on the other side of Saddler. His face had turned even paler.

He found Liencer waiting for him, and they trotted toward the chow hall together. "Was he kidding?" Sullivan asked.

"Who? Kovacs or Hungerford?" Liencer answered.

"Both of them, I guess. What kind of army is this, anyhow? And what's this business about labor battalions?"

Liencer looked at him and shook his head. He grinned

fleetingly. "Sullivan, there's only one place worse than the army, and that's a labor bat. That's where you wind up when you can't pull your weight here. You figure it out. You don't get in the army in the first place if they can figure out a way to fit you in any place besides. But there's some work that takes nothin' but a strong back—a real strong back—and nothin' else. So you figure out what a labor battalion must be like, and then you know how come a guy will bust his tail tryin' to stay in the army.

"If it's punishment details that's got you wonderin', you oughtta know I'm a lucky man. Hungerford's the only sergeant I know of that'll bother to give you a warnin'."

Liencer tapped Sullivan's arm. "So you better stick with me, Sullivan. I know my way around."

Sullivan nodded as they went into the messhall. It looked like Liencer was going to be a good friend.

He and Liencer huddled close to the ground, their heads down, while the cannon shells streamed over them. They were fused to burst just safely behind the half of the company that was on the receiving end, but the gunners were no better at their trade than the men they were firing at, and once Sullivan heard a scream from one of the men behind him.

A lateral burst of fire from one of the automatic rifles went shrieking over their backs, and Sullivan pulled himself closer to the ground. "Keep your tails down," Hungerford kept saying over their helmet circuits. "Keep 'em *down!*"

"You mean they always send men down here that don't have any training at all?" Sullivan shouted to Liencer over the noise. He felt funny. The sound of death tearing the air inches away from him was frightening. But it was the kind of fright that intoxicated him.

74

He could see that Liencer, under his experienced boredom, was pale and sweating, and he couldn't quite understand it. But what he wanted most to find out, right now, was the answer to his question.

"That's right." Liencer grinned with nervous wolfishness. "No sense wasting time on somebody that's gonna turn out dumb enough to get himself killed. Maybe they figure it's good training by itself."

"How long does this keep up?"

"Not much longer. Pretty soon we'll change sides, and we'll be the ones that's pinning *them* down." Liencer's mouth jerked. "Pretty soon Hungerford's going to order us to start pluggin' grenades at their positions. We're supposed to try and make 'em fall short. It ain't so bad if we don't, though. They're pretty well sandbagged in and roofed over. Firing side never loses more'n one to pinned-down side's six. They'll tell you that in tactics class. Holds good in combat, too, or so they tell me. Of course, that's with armor, so it makes up for firing side's not bein' so protected and everybody shootin' for keeps. You gotta learn in this army," he shouted over the crash and whine above them. "A awful lot."

During the grenade throwing, a man somewhere farther down the line got his arm almost completely cut off by MG fire. Afterward, the pinned-down side changed positions with the firing side, and Sullivan and Liencer were assigned to a 20 millimeter cannon.

Hungerford paced back and forth in a slit trench behind their platoon's firing pits, pouring out a stream of instructions, and Kovacs, taking another officer's place behind a permanent machine gun pit with its own specialist crew, kept up a steady chant:

"Those are Moles down there! Hit 'em! Hit 'em!"

The chant and Hungerford's orders streamed into the platoon's helmet phones, and never stopped.

Sullivan and Liencer fired down over the flattened men on the other side of the field, with Sullivan feeding the belt through the cannon, listening bewilderedly to the rising and falling storm of words.

"Traverse! Damn it, traverse those guns! Short bursts! Short bursts and traverse! Get lower with that fire! Come on, you miserable goons, get down as far as you can on those blocks! Come on, *push* those barrels down!"

"Hit 'em! Hit 'em! Hit 'em! Rip the stinking Moles to pieces!"

The cannon shells were exploding almost on top of the men. Sullivan, with his amateur's eye, couldn't understand why the rows of helpless men lying down there weren't being combed into bloody shreds. Liencer had the gun barrel down as far as the safety blocks would let him.

"Hit 'em! Hit 'em!"

"Get lower with that fire, you chicken-hearted jerks! They were giving it to you! Now let them get some of it! Go on! And *swing* those guns! You'll learn about fields of fire later. Now, *short* bursts!"

"Hit 'em! Hit the dirty Moles!"

"Liencer!" Sullivan yelled, "What the hell *is* this?"

Liencer threw a sideward look out of a face that was set in a ghastly grin. "This is trainin', Sullivan. This is where they separate the men from the boys. Get used to it. Get to like it. It's better if you get to like it."

"All right, now," Hungerford was saying, "they're gonna start throwin' grenades in a minute. Hold hard, and keep firing."

"Here they go!" Kovacs shouted. "Keep it up! Pour it on 'em!"

Down in the slight hollow where the other half of the company lay, Sullivan saw men twisting awkwardly to get their grenades out and primed. He stared in fascination as one man raised his shoulder too high and the fabric of his jacket exploded into red all along his upper arm.

"Liencer! You hit that guy!"

Liencer spat. "Yeah. I hope Kovacs saw who did it."

Then the grenades started coming, some of them exploding in the air short of the firing positions, others bouncing along the ground until they blew open and threw dirt over the flaming gun muzzles. The firing slackened involuntarily, and Sullivan, in the middle of ducking away from a hail of gravel and earth, saw Kovacs jump beside the gunner on the specialist MG crew, and point. The gunner fired one burst, and a man who'd got careless when the firing died down suddenly went backward like somebody falling into a pool. The live grenade fell out of his hand and exploded beside him.

"All right!" Kovacs shouted. "Cease firing!"

And the storm of gun fire came to an end. The morning's exercises were over.

They ate chow in the field, lying on their sides and spooning bad food out of their mess kits, ignoring the truck that came out to pick up the casualties. Sullivan listened for anyone talking about what they'd gone through, but didn't hear a word. The old soldiers ate stolidly. The young ones were white-lipped and silent. In a few knots of old soldiers there were brief conversations about women and occasional remarks about the food.

"I don't get it," Sullivan said to Liencer. "What're they after? What's the sense of killing a man or two every day?"

Liencer shrugged. "All I know is, this is the way it's been the last two months. When the Venusians started

77

shippin' out here, that was about the time they started buildin' up the army. They get most of their new blood from the Venusians, but that's only because there's any number of 'em that's too scrawny or too beat-out to work. They had a real rough deal there, they tell me. Anyhow, it ain't just the Venusians. It's native-born citizens, too. If a guy's too weak or too stupid or too sick to work on setting up one of the factories, boom!—he's in the army. There's new ones coming in every day. The idea is, they get themselves killed or banged up so bad they go into a labor bat, or else they just naturally turn into good soldiers. Don't kid yourself—us guys from the old army are good men, even if it was just a little constabulary outfit. We're in the platoon puttin' just enough starch in it to keep it going, until some of these goons learn some soldierin' for themselves."

Sullivan grunted. He couldn't figure out *why* all this was going on. "Yeah—but, look, Liencer, what's it all for? Who's this army going to fight?"

Liencer looked at him, a little wide-eyed. Then he grinned crookedly. "Well—nobody's said anything official. There's a lot of people who figure they don't need any official word. There's a lot of what you might call guessin', if you follow me. But there ain't no sense worryin' about it until the time comes. Nobody else does. You just stick with me. I won't steer you wrong."

Sullivan frowned. That sounded comforting—having somebody to do your worrying for you. And yet somehow it seemed like taking an easy way out.

But he was grateful Liencer was around to keep him from getting his head shot off until he learned to take care of himself.

During the afternoon, Kovacs and Hungerford marched them out to the bayonet dummies. First Hungerford had Saddler show them how. Saddler whipped his bayonet out of his belt, fixed it with a lightning-fast flip of his hand, and charged the nearest dummy with a full-throated bellow. He jammed the blade in, ripped it out, and gave the dummy the butt for good measure. He bayoneted the dummy again, slashing it laterally so the ticking spilled out of the burlap padding, whirled, and charged the next dummy. He stopped just short of lunging at it, and looked inquiringly at Hungerford.

"All right, Saddler," the sergeant said. "Back to your position. Now, the rest of you men; that's how it's done. You go in hard, you go in under the ribs, and you rip. And you yell. You yell hard. O.K.—you!" He pointed at one of the new men. "You try it."

The new man licked his lips and tried to imitate Saddler's dexterity. He fumbled around the barrel of his rifle with the bayonet, finally got it right while Hungerford watched in disgust, and charged the dummy with a cracked yell, his face tense. He missed the forward curve of padding, jabbed his bayonet through the burlap and hit the wooden post at an oblique angle. The rifle wrenched around in his hands, and the butt caught him across the ribs with a dull sound. The man staggered, freed his bayonet, yelled even more feebly and foolishly, and tried to rip the sacking, but only snagged his point.

Hungerford cursed and pushed him back into the ranks. Kovacs paced forward.

"You men! You men are here to learn the bayonet. Sergeant Hungerford is here to teach the bayonet. You will learn the bayonet, you jackasses, one way or the other! You will put your hearts, backs and souls into it. You will *love* that bayonet! You will yell when you jam it in because you *love* to jam it in! You will yell because you *hate* what you destroy with your bayonet! You will cultivate that attitude. You will *charge*, and you will *jam* it in there, and *rip* it out, and you will by God *yell!* Carry on, sergeant." He wiped the back of his hand across his mouth.

They charged the dummies, and they yelled. Sullivan wrapped his big hands around his rifle and swung his shoulders, enjoying the jolt and the sound of sackcloth ripping, while Hungerford shouted corrections and Kovacs stood to one side, shouting:

"Rip 'em! Rip 'em! Rip the dirty Moles! Hate 'em! Yell! Pour it on 'em! *Yell!*"

IX

Sullivan came padding out of the latrine that night, wiping himself dry after his shower. He got to his bunk, and saw that Liencer had put his dirty fatigues away for him and broken out the clean ones.

He grunted his thanks, and Liencer said, "Don't mention it," with a quick grin. "If we're gonna be buddies, that's what buddies are for."

"Yeah—well, thanks anyway," Sullivan said gruffly. He climbed into his clean uniform and began pulling his socks on.

"Hey, mind if I give you a tip?" Liencer asked.

"Go ahead," Sullivan said, looking up.

"Well, you ought to get yourself some shower clogs. You know, wooden ones, so you don't get athlete's foot.".

"Oh, yeah? I didn't know that." He frowned over it. There were all kinds of things he didn't know about.

"Yeah, you really ought to. Believe me, you're gonna be using your feet a lot in this army. Best idea's to keep 'em in good shape."

"Sure."

"Look—tell you what. Let's go over to the canteen. You can pick up a set, and we can down a couple of brews."

A warm, good feeling touched Sullivan. Here was Liencer, one of the old, experienced soldiers, wanting to go out and drink with him, when he could just as easily have asked one of his old friends. He kept his eyes on the floor for a minute, ashamed to let Liencer see the grateful look in them. There was a lot about being in the army that puzzled him; a lot about this one day in it that he couldn't quite understand. But Liencer's invitation made up for it.

"Good idea," he said, and Liencer slapped his shoulder.

"Attaboy, Sullivan!"

They pushed through the canteen doors. The small room was crowded with tables, and the tables were crowded with men sitting around them. There was a steady drone of voices, and an occasional laugh cutting through it. There were men bunched around the small bar in one corner, picking up bottles and paying for them, and carrying them back to the tables.

Liencer led him over to the counter on the opposite side of the canteen. He bought his clogs, and then he and Liencer went over to the bar. It was packed tight. Sullivan couldn't even see it past the men.

Liencer said "Look—s'pose you wait here. I'll shove in there and get ours."

"O.K."

"Right!" Liencer ducked into the jam of men, wiggling and pushing another man a little to one side. He got a hand through to the bar, and a minute later he pulled his way out, holding two beers by their necks.

"Hah! It was a tough fight, but I got 'em." He handed one to Sullivan.

"Thanks. How much do I owe you?"

"Forget it! It's on me. Tomorrow night's yours."

Sullivan shrugged uncomfortably and put his money back in his pocket. He didn't like the thought of Liencer spending some of the little bit of cash pay he got on beers for him. But—well, he'd buy tomorrow night.

He looked around, trying to find an empty table to sit down at. There weren't any, but he did see one with men he recognized from his platoon.

"Hey, you suppose they'd make room for us?" he asked Liencer.

Liencer looked at the men. They were all new recruits. He twitched his mouth. "Looks to me like they're about to leave. That'll give us the whole table. I'll go over and ask 'em." He walked away quickly, and Sullivan saw him leaning over the table.

One of the recruits looked up sharply at Liencer, and Sullivan saw him get an incredulous expression on his face. The other men looked up, too, breaking off their conversation, and one of them said something to Liencer, but Sullivan couldn't hear it. They looked a little angry.

Liencer jerked his thumb over his shoulder, in Sullivan's direction, and the men's eyes shifted toward him. They looked at him expressionlessly, and Sullivan looked back the same way. If one of them had smiled, he would have smiled back. Then all of them looked at Liencer again, and wordlessly picked up their bottles and pushed their chairs back. They walked out the door, carrying their beer, and Liencer looked at Sullivan with a grin. He waved for Sullivan to come over, and Sullivan carried his beer to the table.

"That was pretty nice of them," he said to Liencer, sitting down.

"Yeah." Liencer was looking down at his beer and grinning to himself about something. "I figured they might just be ready to finish their brews outside. So I asked 'em if you and me could have this table. So they said sure." He raised his bottle. "Well, drink up!"

Sullivan smiled at him. "Right!" He tilted his bottle and took a swallow.

The taste of beer took a little getting used to, Sullivan thought, sitting and taking a drink from one of the new bottles Liencer had brought back, but it wasn't bad. It was cold, anyway, and it felt good at the end of the day.

He looked across the table at Liencer and grinned.

Liencer winked back. "How you doin', Sullivan?"

"O.K., I guess." He grinned again. He felt loose and relaxed, and there was a steady, warm trickle of good feeling running through him. He thought back to Small, and thought again that Doncaster's president *had* actually done him a favor by robbing him. Because this *was* what he'd been looking for: good friends, and the ability to relax; and really to be doing something instead of just watching figures change on a tally board. He could sit and drink with a man and look him in the eye, and not be worried about anything. Pretty soon he'd be a good soldier, with Liencer to help him along, and after five years he'd be out, with his own land and a place in the community. Sure, they were rough on you out here, but they had to be. And he was built to take it.

He took another swallow and stretched his legs out comfortably. His ribs felt fine—he'd taken the tape off in the shower tonight—and the soreness in his muscles had been worked out during the day. There was a new hardness in his belly, where the muscles were turning into a tough shield.

He thought about Craddock and Jones for a few minutes. That had been a pretty close thing. If he'd let them push him around, none of the other men would have respected him the way they did now. Probably, Liencer wouldn't want to be his buddy. He felt a little sorry for having banged them up so badly they were sent down to a labor bat, but he hadn't known they would be. And Craddock had really been giving him the works.

That brought him to what Hungerford had said to him last night, and Sullivan frowned a little in puzzlement. He still couldn't make sense out of it. Nobody had started any fights today. If they had, he would have had to do something about it. But they were leaving him alone. They were respecting him—that was all he wanted. After a while they'd all be good friends of his, when they saw he was trying to be a good soldier and a regular guy, and that would be that.

Sure, he admitted he might have lost his head a little last night. But it felt good to know you were just as good a man as anybody else. Nobody could blame you for that.

He finished his beer.

Liencer looked at his watch. "Whaddaya say, Sullivan? You wanna go back to the barracks and play some cards?"

Sullivan smiled broadly. "Sure!" he said.

Liencer winked. "O.K. Let's go." They pushed their chairs back and left the canteen.

Back in the barracks, Sullivan put his shower clogs away while Liencer got a deck of cards out of his own locker and took them over to the table under the overhead bulb at the far wall. Sullivan locked up and crossed the barracks. He saw the bunch of men who'd given them their table in the canteen, sitting around their bunks and talking. He flipped a hand and grinned at them, but they only dropped their eyes and looked down, saying something or other he couldn't quite hear.

He shrugged, feeling a little hurt. He wondered what

they had against him. He sat down thoughtfully, but Liencer kidded him out of his mood.

"Hey, there, Sullivan! Don't go getting down in the mouth even before Professor Liencer shuffles the cards. What'll it be?"

He grinned, feeling good again. This was the kind of man-to-man joshing back and forth he'd only heard other men share. He guessed Ingels and that fellow with the ship from Venus talked to each other like that. He wished he could have kept that date with Ingels last night. He wished he and Ingels and Liencer and Ingels' friend could have got together tonight.

"Tell you the truth, Liencer, it ain't gonna make much difference," he admitted. "Card games are most likely a lot different, back where I come from."

Liencer shrugged. "So what? I'll teach you. And don't worry about the money, either." He winked. "I don't play for money with my friends. How's about some casino?"

Sullivan's eyes lit up. He *did* know how to play casino. He and his father had played it quite frequently at home for recreation.

"That's one you ain't gonna hafta show me," he growled. "Deal!"

They played for a few minutes, with Sullivan relaxed and enjoying himself. When the outside door opened, down near the middle of the barracks, he looked up idly to see who'd come in.

"Who's that?" Liencer asked.

"Saddler."

A slow grin spread across Liencer's face. "No kiddin'? I figured it might be. I saw him in the canteen."

"Maybe we should of asked him to sit with us."

Liencer's grin widened. "I figured maybe I'd ask him to join our game." He turned in his chair. "Saddler! Hey, Saddler!"

Saddler's head jerked, and he looked coldly at Liencer. "Yes?" Sullivan could see he was surprised at Liencer's speaking to him. Sullivan frowned, trying to figure it out.

"Wanna play some cards with me and my buddy Sullivan?" There was a peculiar edge in Liencer's voice, and Sullivan looked at him quickly, feeling bewildered.

Saddler's eyes flicked over Sullivan and went back to Liencer. "No."

The edge in Liencer's voice grew broader. "My buddy, here, is pretty anxious for you to play cards with us, Saddler."

Saddler's chest heaved in a sigh. He came toward the table and stopped, looking down at Liencer. But Sullivan was almost positive Saddler was keeping tabs on him, too, out of the corner of his eye.

"Liencer, I never cared for your company before, and I don't care for it now, whether he's your buddy or not."

Sullivan looked at the two of them, lost. There was some kind of tension between them, but he couldn't understand it. He noticed the barracks had quieted down completely, and he kept his eyes locked on the two of them.

Liencer grinned up at Saddler. "You mean," he said softly, "you don't like my buddy?"

Saddler took a step back and said: "Let's get it straight, Liencer." He was looking at Sullivan now, though, his eyes cautious. "I didn't say anything about Sullivan. I don't like you, and I never have. You're a bum soldier, and you're a barracks lawyer. I don't like your attitude, and I wouldn't play cards with you any more than I'd just hand you my money. Is that clear? Now, if your buddy wants me to play, that makes a difference by this much; I'm going to get into something I don't want to. But I still won't play cards with you." His eyes on Sullivan were still cautious, but they were as steady as his voice.

Sullivan was completely out of his depth. He couldn't put his finger on *what* was going on around here.

"Never mind the cracks about me!" Liencer flared. "What you're sayin' is you won't play with Sullivan because he's a Mole. Right?" He jerked his head around and looked angrily at Sullivan. He spat: "You gonna let him get away with that?"

Sullivan's eyes were troubled. A few minutes ago, he'd been relaxed and feeling good. Now this. He wished Liencer hadn't put it that way. He liked Saddler—Saddler was a good, quiet soldier.

He saw Saddler watching him. "Now—wait a minute, Liencer," he said slowly, "Saddler didn't say anything to me, yet."

Liencer looked at him in disbelief. "You really gonna let him get away with it?"

Sullivan shook his head. "Look—all the guy said was he didn't want to play cards, and he doesn't like you. Seems to me that's his privilege." It all puzzled Sullivan—particularly because he liked Liencer and Saddler both, though Saddler not as much as Liencer, of course, since he didn't know him. But he could see where a man had a right to a mistaken opinion, and he didn't think that was any reason to get upset at Saddler.

Saddler and Liencer were both looking at him with different kinds of surprise. Then Saddler laughed in Liencer's face and walked away.

Liencer swept his hand across the table and threw the cards aside. He glared at Sullivan for a minute, and then he kicked his chair back and stood up. He looked like he was going to say something, and then he didn't.

"Look . . ." Sullivan tried to think of a way of explaining to him. But he didn't even know for sure what Liencer was mad about. "Take it easy, Liencer." He moved his hands awkwardly. "I appreciate you looking out for me, but Saddler didn't mean anything by it. He just—well, he just didn't want to play cards, I guess. I know he said some pretty raw things to you, but you can't expect everybody to like you." He saw he wasn't making himself very clear, and stopped. "Look—sit down. Play some casino. Take your mind off it."

Liencer sat down. They played for a while, but the spirit was gone out of the game, with Liencer scowling silently at his cards and Sullivan troubled. When lights out came, they climbed into their bunks without saying anything important. Sullivan stayed awake for a long time, trying to decide whether he'd done the right thing or not. He couldn't make up his mind, and fell asleep still unhappy.

When reveille woke him up in the morning, he dropped over the side of his bunk and looked anxiously at Liencer, to see if he was still in a bad mood.

"Liencer—look—I'm sorry about last night," he said, trying to straighten it out.

Liencer surprised him by grinning broadly and slapping his back. "Forget it, Sullivan! It's O.K. I thought about it some, and I can see why you didn't cream that crud, Saddler. You're new here. You don't know. Believe me, that guy's poison. He's been on my back ever since we came into this platoon. Nothing satisfies him. He's one of these guys, you know, if you don't do things the way *he* figgers they ought to be, you're no good."

"Oh." Sullivan frowned. "I didn't know that. I just figured he was a good soldier."

"Well, believe me, there's lots better than Saddler. Lots. But it's O.K. You just listen to ol' Flash from now on, and I'll steer you on who's a good guy around here and who isn't. You forget about Saddler for the time bein'. Now—let's hit those showers before we get caught late for roster."

88

He chuckled suddenly, and slapped Sullivan's back again as they headed for the latrine. "Boy, you notice he didn't want any part of tangling with you! You're all right, Sullivan! Yes, sir, you're a good buddy to have."

Sullivan grinned with relief. He was glad Liencer hadn't kept last night's black mood.

When he formed up for roster, he moved into his spot beside Saddler with his face expressionless. Saddler looked at him, and looked like he might have started to say something. But Sullivan kept his face blank and his eyes level. Saddler twitched one shoulder, grunted and faced front.

Goodwin read the roster, and Kovacs gave them their morning pep talk. Hungerford stepped forward and told them they were going to learn unarmed combat in the morning and go to tactics class in the afternoon and dismissed them for chow.

All through his breakfast, Sullivan found himself looking forward to the morning's work. Nobody knew better than he that he didn't know the first thing about taking care of himself. There were going to be times when just raw strength wasn't going to be enough. He'd have to know how to use it; how to channel it so it would do the most good.

The company marched out to the exercise field, and Sullivan realized his body had already sharpened up a good bit. Some of the recruits who'd been in the platoon for weeks were looking a little winded by the time they'd marched out to the exercise field. Sullivan had fallen into an easy, swinging stride, and the march was just enough to tune him up and take out the few kinks left over from yesterday's work. When he reached the field he was relaxed and ready, his muscles loose. He watched attentively while two of the specialist instructors demonstrated holds, and when his platoon's turn came to be paired off with the instructors, he grinned a tight, anticipatory grin and pitched in.

It was rough work. His opponent was an instructor named Gandy, with incredibly fast hands and no mercy. For the first few minutes, he had Sullivan dazed and staggering. Sullivan heard a few watching men from another platoon laugh at him after a particularly bad spill. He got up with a crooked smile of his own, knowing he must have looked pretty silly. But he went back at it, trying to keep up with the movements of Gandy's feet and guess where the next attack would come from. Gandy's eyes, he'd found out the hard way, weren't any help. The man could look over your shoulder and sink two fingers exactly into your solar plexus at the same time.

He caught on, gradually. His reflexes learned new cues, and his reactions came quicker and nearer to being right as he learned what to do with his muscles.

The first time Gandy tried an attack and he blocked it, he almost laughed out loud. He tried a hold of his own, and Gandy threw him, but he bounced back to his feet with a growl that burst spontaneously out of his throat and had nothing to do with anger. He was finding out that his body, given a chance, could develop a brain of its own, and react with a speed quicker than conscious thought. With his muscles humming, and the growl purring in his chest, he charged in at Gandy, feinted and shot out a hand that spun the instructor over his outstretched leg. Gandy twisted in mid-air and kicked him down, but when they both came jumping back to their feet again, the instructor was grinning.

They kept it up for another ten minutes, and halfway through them Sullivan tried a complicated hold he'd seen demonstrated, and Gandy went down while Sullivan stayed on his feet. It didn't happen again, but when the whistle blew Gandy pulled him up and nodded shortly. "Pretty good. What's your name, bud?"

Sullivan told him, and Gandy stuck out his hand. "You're going to be an all-right man, Sully."

Sullivan grinned with pure pleasure, putting his shirt back on. He looked around, and saw most of the other trainees lying on the ground, panting. One of them had a broken collarbone. Another one was flopping around with his hands over his belly. He saw with surprise that it was one of the old soldiers, and then he realized just how wonderfully good he ought to be feeling.

During the afternoon, Sullivan and Liencer had sat together through tactics class, learning what an automatic rifleman did in relation to the MG gunners, and how a 20mm gunner covered an advance and handled an assault from the flank. Liencer had sat there bored, and Sullivan had been listening with half his attention while the other half of his mind and his restless muscles reminded him of the morning.

When the class ended, Liencer stood up, stretched and tapped Sullivan on the arm. "Glad that's over. Well, let's go, Sullivan. Let's hit that chow line. I could eat the sling off Hungerford's carbine."

"Ain't that what we had for lunch?" Sullivan cracked, feeling happy about the whole day, and glad that Liencer hadn't taken any offense about last night. Liencer laughed, and they went over to the field kitchen, griping about the food, the seats in the prefab where the class was held, the cold and the lack of hot water in the showers, like a couple of hardened old troopers.

They came up to the long line of men stretching away from the kitchen, with Sullivan still busy at his feeling of really belonging; of being a respected man for the first time in the forty-nine years of his life. He opened his mess kit automatically, and started for the end of the line, but Liencer touched his arm.

"Nuts to that. Time we get to the food, it'll be cold as Kovacs's heart. There's some of the boys from the platoon, up near the kitchen. Come on."

Sullivan followed Liencer as he cut toward the head of the line. Liencer walked up to the men, who, Sullivan saw, were some of the men who'd given up their table in the canteen last night.

"Hey, there, how's about making some room for my buddy and me?" He turned back to Sullivan. "Come on. Slide in there." Sullivan followed the pull of his arm, starting a smile and a "Thanks" toward the man he was getting in front of. When the man said, in a strained, high voice: "Get the hell back to the end of the line, Ape!" Sullivan stared at him with his mouth hanging open.

Liencer shouldered his way forward. "What'd you say?"

The man dropped his mess kit and stood there pale-faced, the corners of his mouth trembling, while the line jammed to a stop behind him. He was one of the scrawny, high-strung Venusian recruits. His eyes were wide with the flare of some furious emotion.

"I've had all I'm gonna take from you two!" he shouted. The rest of the men with him were staring at him and then back to Sullivan in panic. They shuffled backward, pushing against the pressure of the line behind them, leaving the three of them standing alone. "I don't care! I don't care how goddam big you are!" he yelled at Sullivan, "I've had enough of it!"

"All right, punk," Liencer said in a flat voice. He stepped aside and pushed Sullivan forward. "Go on, Sullivan," he said. "Teach this wise guy."

Sullivan looked from Liencer to the Venusian and back again. How had *this* happened? He wasn't sure what to do. He remembered last night, with Saddler, and looked at Liencer uncertainly. He didn't want to make another mistake.

Liencer pushed him again. "Go on, Sullivan! Take care of him!"

Sullivan was still holding on to his mess kit. He was wondering what had got the Venusian so worked up, when the Venusian suddenly made a strangled noise and swung at him. He felt a dull crunch in his nose, and a streak of incredible pain shot across his eyes and blinded him for a moment. He put his hand up to his face and swung his other arm. He felt his mess kit hit the other man, and heard him go down. He stepped back, his eyes slowly clearing, with blood running down his chin, and looked at the Venusian lying there with a puffed gash across his scalp. The recruit's hands were twitching, and he was trying to roll over.

Liencer looked at the rest of the men from their platoon. "Ya satisfied? Ya found out for good who's boss in our barracks?" Sullivan looked down at the recruit, wondering if he'd done the right thing.

X

SULLIVAN CAME down the company street, released from the hospital, his nose packed and taped, squinting down the darkness between the buildings. Both his eyes were swollen and black, and there was a steady ache in the front of his head that chewed through the shot of anesthetic he'd been given. He saw somebody standing in front of the day room door, and peered at him.

He saw it was Goodwin, standing there watching him, and started to go past him to the door straight into the barracks.

93

"Not in there, Sullivan," Goodwin said. "Hungerford wants to see you."

"O.K.," Sullivan said, feeling his skull twinge to the vibration of the words. He looked at Goodwin to see if there was anything more he wanted to say, but the corporal had turned and was walking toward the barracks door. Sullivan went up into the day room, through it to Hungerford's door, and knocked.

"Come on in," Hungerford said, and Sullivan pushed the door open. Hungerford was sitting behind his desk, his feet on his wastebasket, with the bottle in his hand. "Shut the door," Hungerford said, and then looked up. "Well, you're a pretty sight." He went back to staring over his desk with bloodshot eyes.

Sullivan stood beside the desk, waiting for whatever it was that Hungerford wanted to say, watching him take a quick gulp out of the bottle. He followed his line of sight, and saw he was staring at the Feurmann print across the room.

"Quit gawking at that!" Hungerford's voice startled him, and he snapped his head back toward the sergeant. "It's mine. You keep your eyes where they belong." He took another drink. "You know something, Sullivan? It's about officers. They take a written examination at officers' school. An old lieutenant of mine named Corwin told me about it. They have all sorts of hypothetical questions thrown at them. Like: suppose the halliards on the flagpole are snarled and it's impossible to lower the flag at sunset. You're in charge of a detail with a sergeant and some men. What order do you give? Answer: 'Sergeant, get up that pole.'" Hungerford put his bottle down on the desk. "So when Kovacs gets told to turn out a cadre of seasoned non-coms, fast, I get up that pole. Lean against the wall if you want to, Sullivan. You may be here a while."

Sullivan stared at him. He wondered how long Hungerford had been sitting here alone, taking down the level in that bottle.

"All right, Sullivan, forget that. I know all about what happened on the chow line tonight. You came close to doing me a favor. A little harder, and it would have been one more man in the hospital and then down to the labor battalion. He swung first—you shouldn't have been able to down him after that. This is a pragmatic army. Well, don't do me those favors, Sullivan. I do my own favors, or Kovacs lends a hand." He looked up. "What appened in the canteen last night?"

"I don't think I follow you, sergeant."

"Who went over and chased those men away from their table?"

"Nobody chased them. They were ready to go."

"So Liencer went over, right? And Liencer tried to buck the chow line tonight. Right?" He looked at Sullivan. "I wondered how your bunk got itself made up so well." He looked down at his desk and smiled crookedly. "I could have stood for another Craddock. Kovacs likes them. But not the team. I'll be damned if I'm going to have another Jones. What about that fight Liencer tried to pick for you and Saddler?"

Sullivan was completely lost under the impact of one sharp sentence after another. He couldn't understand half of what Hungerford was saying. He just shook his head. He wished he knew more about living this kind of life. Maybe what Hungerford was saying would make sense then.

"You don't get it, do you? I told you the other night— you fell into a perfect spot to make a damned fool of yourself. You didn't waste any time at it, did you?"

Hungerford pushed himself up in his chair. "I'll spell it out." He jerked his head in the direction of the barracks. "Liencer's an operator. He knows how to soldier, but he won't soldier. He's a conniver. He doesn't gamble for relaxation, he gambles for money. He doesn't have friends, he has stooges. Liencer never does anything without calculating how much good it's going to do him. Is that plain enough?"

Sullivan shook his head again.

"Liencer hates Saddler's guts. Saddler called him on some kind of deal, one day, and told him what he'd do to him if he ever tried it again. Now, what do you suppose Liencer's been thinking about, in relation to Saddler, ever since then?"

It finally got through to Sullivan. He stood there in Hungerford's office, and asked:

"Are the rest of the men in the platoon scared of me? Besides Saddler?"

Hungerford snorted. "Saddler's possibly the one man who isn't, though I wouldn't bet on it. I *would* bet on his going up against you if he had to. Look, Sullivan—you're a big hefty bruiser, which is bad enough. But you don't know anything about fighting a man. You don' know when you're beaten, and you don't know what to use to hit with, and you don't know when to stop. That's the worst part of it. That's what frightens experts. Only a dumb fool like that kid in the chow line would tackle you without giving it a great deal of thought."

Sullivan took a deep breath, and his face twisted into a contorted smile. "All right, Hungerford. Thanks."

"Sergeant Hungerford, soldier," Hungerford said, surprisingly grinning back in almost the same way. He raised his bottle and added: "O.K., Sullivan, now get out of here and think of something to do to square yourself. And let me get back to my drinking."

A flash of illogical liking for the man made Sullivan suddenly feel that he ought to explain what had happened. He gestured awkwardly. "I—well, all I wanted them to do was respect me!" He surprised himself with the pathetic note in his voice.

Hungerford looked at him and shook his head sadly. Then a frustrated expression crossed his own face, and he cursed in an undertone. He said "Damn it, Sullivan, I should have told you sooner. I should have thought of what putting you that close to Liencer would result in. But you caught me by surprise. And I suppose I had to put you somewhere in that barracks, so I guess there was no helping it." He took another drink. "I usually let a man go to hell in his own way. It's my principal commandment, and the only one I haven't broken. Very often. It's a very good one, for this pragmatic army. Get out of here, Sullivan, I'm going to be begging your pardon in a minute." He sank down in his chair and went back to looking at his picture.

Sullivan closed the door behind him. He found a chair in the dark day room, and sat down.

Liencer—this whole situation—was something out of a nightmare, and he didn't know what to do.

He winced inside himself at the thought of how Liencer had curried his friendship and shrewdly used his naïveté to give him a completely wrong picture of things. When he remembered how anxious he'd been to make it up to Liencer for not doing his dirty work, he twisted in the chair and beat his fist against his thigh. He thought about how the men in the barracks must feel about Liencer's ordering them around in his name, and he knew he had to do something.

He'd thought he was becoming one of them. He'd thought they respected him for handling Craddock and Jones. He'd felt like one of them, and he'd wanted to be part of the platoon. He hadn't understood the picture of him in their minds.

He had to show them it hadn't been his fault. He had to think of some way to prove, once and for all, that it hadn't been he, but Liencer, that had created this situation.

Finally, he thought of something. He got up and crossed the day room. He opened the door from the day room into the barracks, and stepped inside.

He saw the men sitting on their bunks raise their faces toward him and then drop them. He saw Liencer lying on his bunk, his hands behind his head, with a light smile on his face. He walked over to the foot of Liencer's bunk and said: "Stand up, Liencer."

"Huh? Hey, buddy, you teed off about something?" Liencer looked at him worriedly for a moment. Then the broad grin flashed across his face. "What's the matter, pal? Hungerford chew you out?" His eyes were wary.

Sullivan felt himself move before he even thought about it. He pulled Liencer off his bunk and slammed him back against their lockers. He cracked his hand across Liencer's face.

"Stay away from me from now on," he growled. "Stay away from me and keep your mouth shut. You say one word to me and I'll make you wish you never heard of me." He threw him back on his bunk and faced the barracks, waiting for somebody to say something to show he'd done the right thing.

But nobody said anything. They looked at him coldly as he turned his head, bewildered, his eyes going from face to face. He saw the thin recruit watching him, lying on his bunk with a taped bandage across his scalp. He walked over to him. He started to say "Look, I'm sorry. It wasn't my fault."

The recruit looked up at him, white-faced. "Get away from me, you crazy ape," he said shrilly before Sullivan could open his mouth. "Go back and beat your buddy up some more."

Sullivan turned again, and the men's eyes were following him. He walked toward Saddler's bunk, and saw Saddler watching him, his eyes careful, with a piece of one-by-two in his hand.

"Look—Saddler . . ."

"Go to bed, Sullivan," Saddler told him. He didn't move off his bunk, but he held the piece of lumber ready. Sullivan found himself wondering what he'd intended to do with it, originally. He must have picked it up before Sullivan came back into the barracks.

Sullivan tried again. He turned away from Saddler and toward Goodwin's bunk, and then, before he ever even actually looked at the corporal, he realized it was no use. Somehow, he had moved too far away.

He stood in the middle of the barracks, not moving, with an overhead bulb glaring down on him and the men watching from their shadowy bunks. Liencer was lying face-down, his hands knotted in his blanket, motionless.

He saw, with stabbing clarity, that he had somehow trapped himself. His shoulders started to sag, and he jerked them back, conscious of the eyes on him. If he let them see they had him down, they might do almost anything to him.

He hoisted himself up into his bunk and lay there in his clothes. It was quiet in the barracks until lights out, and then he heard one man after another roll over and fall asleep. He lay awake, his face aching, wiping away a trickle of blood from where the packing had loosened, until it clotted again.

He was completely alone, now. He didn't even have Liencer any more.

After reveille, he got out of his fatigues long enough to take a shower, ignoring the other men and being ignored. He made up his bunk, while a pale and frightened Liencer waited in the latrine until he was through, and then he went out to roster formation. He and Saddler stood shoulder to shoulder, carefully making sure they didn't touch each other, and after formation he ate

99

alone in the messhall. He marched out to the exercise field with the platoon, locked in the shell of himself, and there he took his bayonet practice.

While Kovacs chanted in his overriding voice, Sullivan charged the dummies, and suddenly his throat opened, and he bellowed. He chocked his bayonet through the padding into the posts. He retracted with a jerk of his arms and a leg against the post, and roared, and tore the padding with savage rips of his blade. He charged and yelled, and splintered the posts. He tore the padding into shreds, and roared.

And Lieutenant Kovacs ordered him to drop by his office at the headquarters building that night.

Kovacs in his office was not Kovacs on the practice field. Kovacs in his office was a wiry, perfectly calm man behind a desk, his thumbs and forefingers together. Sullivan noticed the difference, but did not think about it. He stood at attention in front of Kovacs's desk, his eyes dull.

"John L. Sullivan," Kovacs said softly, looking at the pyramid of his hands. "John L. Sullivan. A fascinating name. It fits you, Sullivan."

"Yes, sir."

Kovacs's mouth quirked. "These aren't duty hours, Sullivan. Relax. I have." His mouth moved again into that pursed, faint, ruminative smile. "I've done my shouting for the day. Did you suspect I actually hate raising my voice? But my duties call for it, so I do it. Does what I say surprise you?"

Sullivan only knew that Kovacs must be working toward some point. He wondered what it might be, but he made no attempt to anticipate it. "I don't know, sir."

"*Hmm!*" It was a pleased laugh, entirely private. Kovacs sighed pleasurably and came to the point. "We're building something here, Sullivan. We're building an

100

army second to none. Second to *none* in the Solar System. Do you follow me?"

"No, sir."

Now Kovacs's sudden upward glance was sharp. "You seem to be under some emotional strain. That performance with the bayonet this morning was quite impressive. I might have guessed it was a sort of explosion. *Wasn't* it, Sullivan?"

"I couldn't say, sir."

"And now you've reacted in the opposite direction. Withdrawn. Well, that's all right, too. I like a complex man. You *are* complex, Sullivan. I think something will come of you. You're a superb physical specimen. But, you're intelligent, as well—oh, yes, you *are*, in spite of the condition of your face." Kovacs was once more staring at his hands.

"I called you in here to tell you something. To encourage you. Yes. I'll be brief. One day soon, we'll be looking for officer material. All the pres t o   s will be promoted several grades. The present noncommissioned officer cadre will not suffice to fill the vacated lower ranks. Think about that, Sullivan. Think about whether you'd like being an officer when we move out."

He looked up again. "We *will* be moving out. We're a very poor nation, Sullivan. Frustrated. I do not feel as emotional about it as I may seem on the field, but I do feel it very strongly. I'll want dependable subordinates on that campaign." He put his hands flat on the edge of his desk and half stood up from his chair. His quiet, calm eyes burned into Sullivan's face. "I want to impress that upon you, Sullivan. I want you to remember it clearly, because it is the most important thing in my life, and I will not stand for *anyone's* frustrating me at the critical moment. *I intend to rise in this army, Sullivan. I intend to rise past lieutenant, past captain, past major—past any rank whatsoever that represents anything less than the* very top. Before I have shot my bolt, I intend to be lead-ing this army. Before the war is over, I intend to be the commanding general. And after the war, I intend to build on that structure, and rise to a point where no man no thing, no act of Nature will ever be able to pull me down. Not ever. Is that clear?"

"Yes, sir."

"Good." He sat down and smiled. "I'll want you lead-ing my best platoon when we invade Earth." He looked up at Sullivan, quite quickly. "Surprised?"

Sullivan was thinking that Kovacs somehow reminded him of another man. Earth? Well, now he knew what the army was for. And to be an officer? Sullivan knew Kovacs's intention was to make him ambitious. Probably Sullivan thought, he could feel that way if he tried. Now the thing to do was to react in some way Kovacs would like.

"Yes, sir, I'm surprised."

"And are you with me?"

Without hesitation, he answered the taut whisper. "Yes, sir."

Kovacs sighed, again pleasurably. "Good. I'll be watch-ing you. Dismissed, Sullivan."

Sullivan saluted and excuted as good an about face as he could. He left the headquarters building. On his way to the barracks, he thought without any particular re-action that it was Mr. Small that Kovacs reminded him of.

And he wondered, only idly, what Mr. Small was do-ing these days. What Doncaster might be doing. He wondered, too, idly, if Doncaster would survive the war. It seemed hard to believe that an enterprise like that would permit itself to be snuffed out. Or if, indeed, it could possibly not know about danger to itself long be-fore the danger became apparent. But he wondered only idly.

XI

Sullivan grinned tightly at Gandy, and circled. They'd gone through this eight or ten times in the past two months, and Sullivan had come to look forward to it. As always, lately, most of the men who weren't paired off with instructors were standing in a circular crowd around them, watching quietly. Sullivan saw Gandy flick an annoyed glance at the spectators, and he rumbled a chuckle. Having the men stand around and watch always bothered Gandy. Sullivan didn't mind it. He ignored them.

Gandy came in low, going for the legs, and Sullivan danced aside in the direction he knew Gandy expected. He shifted suddenly, and as Gandy jackknifed up to go for the nerve centers in the thighs, Sullivan caught his wrist and snapped him aside. Gandy rolled twice, bounced to his feet just short of the crowd, gave his arm a shake, and started circling again. He was scowling.

Sullivan chuckled again. So far today, he'd been thrown just once, and he'd kicked Gandy down, too. He moved fluidly in counter to Gandy's next charge, and Gandy broke it off. Sullivan peeled his lips back and growled "'Matter, Gandy?"

Gandy did what Sullivan had expected. He stood up straight, with his hands on his hips, and said "All right, Killer, suppose you come in at me." The corners of his mouth were white, and sunken deep into his cheeks. His voice wasn't quite steady.

Sullivan had realized Gandy's temper was his weakness the second time they paired off. Gandy had smiled and started to shake hands with him, and Sullivan had stared him down. Gandy had gone white, and Sullivan had come close to holding up his end that day. He'd already had the edge in reflexes, and he learned quickly. He learned with a scowling, single-minded concentration.

The next time he'd had the better coordination, too. And the fourth time Sullivan had thrown Gandy more often than Gandy had had him down. After that Sullivan had stopped scowling.

Now he laughed and moved forward. Gandy came to meet him, and Sullivan feinted with his left hand, reached with his right, turned with a kick of his right leg and caught the top of Gandy's shoulder in his left hand. He buried his thumb under the collarbone, brought his stabbing right hand into Gandy's armpit, kicked Gandy's driving leg aside, and brought his right elbow up under Gandy's chin just as the instructor tried to double away.

Gandy, his right arm helpless, twisted like a hooked fish. Sullivan's thumb worked under Gandy's collarbone, and he ground the stiff fingers of his right hand toward the curve of Gandy's fourth rib, lying just under the skin in his armpit. He hooked the first joints of his fingers over it, pushed Gandy forward with the heel of his left hand, and wrenched him around until he was behind Gandy's right shoulder, with Gandy's arm locked between his own upper arm and his chest. He kicked Gandy's feet out from under him, held him for a second, and then let him crumple to the ground. He looked across the small cleared space and saw Goodwin and Saddler watching him, their faces pale. He laughed, and they dropped their eyes. He saw Kovacs standing to one side, looking at him with approval.

Hungerford's whistle blew almost in his ear. "All right, next bunch!" the sergeant yelled, and the crowd broke up toward the instructors. Sullivan noticed that the other instructors were pointedly ignoring Gandy, and were keeping their attention on their own work. He grinned coldly and bent over to pick up his shirt, his back muscles stretching pleasurably.

"Get your kicks for today all right, Sullivan?" Hungerford asked.

Sullivan grunted and buttoned his shirt. He looked down at Gandy, who was just sitting up, holding his right arm tight against his ribs, staring with pain. He hooked his mouth into a wordless grin.

"Well, that just about takes care of everything, doesn't it?" Hungerford persisted. "You've worked yourself into a spot where there's nobody left in this army that'll have the guts to stand up to you."

Sullivan wished Hungerford would stop needling him. He grimaced in annoyance and moved away.

Hungerford was the only man in the army who could say something and have it get through to him. He didn't know why—he'd never worked it out completely. But even when Hungerford was digging at him, the way he had been just now, there was a funny kind of twisted liking in the sergeant's voice. Sometimes Sullivan thought there was some kind of pity, too. He didn't want to be sure, because he would have had to do something about it.

That was the thing of it. Maybe because Hungerford's eyes didn't get cautious and shifty like everybody else's did, and maybe because Hungerford was the one man who'd really tried to do something for him. Sullivan couldn't quite cut himself off from him. And when the times came when, like today, he would have had to do something about it if Hungerford had pushed his line of comment a little further, he found himself giving ground.

Sullivan shook his head at himself and walked over to his platoon. The men left a space around him, and he stood by himself in their midst.

Sullivan lay on his bunk after evening chow, looking off into space. He'd just finished stripping, cleaning and reassembling his equipment, but he was too good at it. It hadn't taken more than a half hour. The other men had a card game going, but Sullivan didn't like watching pinochle.

He rolled over on his back. He still had three hours to lights out. Finally, he dropped down to the floor and got his combat knife out of his locker and went outside, to where one of the lights on the fence around the base shone on the chipped and splintered board he had set up behind the barracks.

Methodically, first underhand and then overhand, he practiced throwing at the board. The heavy knife thunked deep into the wood with each throw, and he trudged up to the board, yanked the knife out, trudged back to his mark, turned and threw again. The dull sound of the knife beat against the barracks wall with clocklike regularity, and his boots gritted on the dirt between each throw.

Gradually, he accelerated the rhythm. His arm snapped forward more quickly, and he walked faster. His movements fell into a closed cycle. Throw, walk up to the board, turn and pull the knife out at the same time, walk back to the mark, turn and throw. The knife thudded into the wood, driving deeper and deeper, until finally some part of the board split, and he shifted his aim.

He began throwing overhand the way trick artists on stage do it, flipping the knife end-over-end. It was a useless thing for a soldier to learn, but he could snap his arm like a whip that way, and feel the jolt travel up to his shoulder as he stopped the arm dead and let the knife fly.

"Sullivan!"

He turned his head. Hungerford had thrown his office

window open. "Have a heart, will you? Come on in here a minute."

Sullivan looked at him angrily, went over and got his knife, and walked around the end of the barracks to get to Hungerford's office. He knocked and opened the door.

Hungerford was sitting alone with his bottle again. Sullivan scowled, and Hungerford said with annoyance: "Put that knife away before you look at me like that." He flipped a card-sized piece of paper toward Sullivan. "Here."

Sullivan dropped his knife into its sheath and picked up the paper.

"That's a ten-hour pass into town. You don't have to be back until reveille. Put your dress blacks on and get out of here."

Sullivan looked at the pass. He hadn't been off the base since the day he'd landed. "Don't do me any favors," he growled.

"You're entitled to it. The other men get them. Beyond that, my motives are simple. I want a little quiet around here, so I can get my drinking done in peace. On both counts, that's no favor. Take the thing. Don't tell me you'd be homesick for this barracks."

Sullivan shook his head doubtfully. He looked at the pass again. He was happy where he was, the way he was.

Hungerford looked at him with that peculiar mixture of liking and pity, and Sullivan twitched his face in annoyance as he looked away.

"Take a walk down some streets," Hungerford said. "See some new faces. Look around at the kind of world you're living in. Get drunk. Go see a movie. Do you need any money?"

Sullivan scowled "No. I've got two months' pay."

"That's right. You don't even spend any time at the

canteen," Hungerford said flatly. "You don't gamble with the men."

Sullivan looked at him, and Hungerford looked steadily back.

"All right," Sullivan said. "Thanks." He walked out of the office, holding the pass gingerly, and into the barracks. He saw the men around the card game lift their heads and drop them quickly, and suddenly he couldn't wait to get out.

Even at night, Port MacDonnel's factories made more noise than its people did. Sullivan, walking down the street toward the center of town, passed building after new building surrounding the few older factories. Some of the new ones were only half finished, and already men were jockeying machinery into place, setting up production lines while contractors worked around them, finishing the plant structure.

He'd shaken his head about that. Ingels had told him these people were short on heavy machinery, and Ingels hadn't had any reason not to tell the truth. He just plain hadn't known. Which meant that all this was something brand new. They must have built their own machines, finally.

It wasn't his business. When the factories were set up and the army was fully equipped, he'd be ready to move with it. That was all there was to it. But he couldn't help thinking about it a little, with machines whining on either hand and the blue flare of welding torches stabbing at his eyes.

He'd learned a few things in the army. He knew, for instance, that there were two ways to build a new machine—run raw materials through a machine for making machines, or else shape the raw materials by hand. The first machine for making machines *had* to be made by hand.

And they wouldn't be turning out just one kind of new machine. So any number of new master machines had had to be hand-built—out of the tough, macrocrystalline metals he'd seen stop a point-blank 22mm shell at the body armor demonstrations. He walked on, wondering at the force of the bitterness that had driven the Plutonians into putting out that much effort with their slim resources. He began to understand why everybody had to work. He wondered at people who could feel so hard about anything.

He shook his head and turned onto Port MacDonnel's short main street, not knowing where he was going or what he was going to do, but walking steadily.

The street was only moderately crowded. There were a few small stores on it, and only a few bars. He passed those without looking in. He didn't have any interest in letting his body go to seed, and he didn't intend to let his mind get dull. The thought of not having perfect control over himself frightened him.

There was one movie house on the street, showing a picture with stars in it who were ten and twenty years dead, some of them. It had to be something brought out from Earth long ago, and re-run and re-run to a point of almost incredible boredom. He jerked his mouth into a grin at the thought of how that house's manager must have felt at the sight of a brand new audience being shipped in from Venus.

But Sullivan certainly didn't want to see it.

He walked a little more tensely, looking around. If you didn't drink, and you didn't want to go to the movies, and you weren't interested in shopping, and if looking at new faces only proved that one group of people looked much like any other, there wasn't a thing to do in town.

He worked his shoulders under his jacket, boredom making him restless, and kept walking only because he

109

wasn't yet ready to lean against a wall with his hands in his pockets. Finally, almost at the end of the street, he saw a small place with a sign that read: "Good Food."

He looked at it for a minute. Maybe it was a lie, but the army didn't even make a pretense. He made up his mind and walked toward it.

The place was just a casual sort of eatery, with a counter and stools. He walked in, sat down at the other end of the counter from some other soldiers who were strangers to him, and looked at the sparse menu printed on the sign behind the counter. He looked for the waitress, and saw her just turning away from the soldiers. She was short, had blond hair, and was pretty in a way, though he thought her face was too long, her lower lip was too thin, and her hands were chapped.

XII

SHE WALKED quickly up the length of the counter, took a glass of water off a tray as she passed it, and set it down in front of him.

"What'll it be, soldier?" she asked in a voice that struck Sullivan as being a little too gruff. She had an air of casual friendliness about her, but he noticed she was sparing with her smile.

He looked at the menu again. "Are you kidding when you say steak?" he asked with a smile.

"It's tough, but a sharp knife goes with it. Rare, medium or well?"

"Medium, please."

"Fried potatoes and beets?"

"That would be fine, thank you."

"Well, you're not hard to please. It'll be a couple of

minutes. Coffee meantime?" She shrugged meaningly. "You Venus boys wouldn't know—it's synthetic. How's about milk?"

He nodded. "That would be fine."

"O.K." She filled a glass and put it down. "I'll be back with that steak in a jiffy."

He watched her go through a door into the kitchen, and watched the door until she came out, carrying an armload of plates for the soldiers at the other end of the counter. He watched them talk to her vehemently while she was putting their orders down, watched her glance toward him and go back into the kitchen. He watched her come out and serve some other customers, and then he watched her go back into the kitchen to pick up his order. He kept his eyes on the menu as she came toward him.

"So you're Killer Sullivan," she said as she put the plate down. He looked up sharply. She grinned back at him. "You don't act like it." She nodded. "But you look like it, all right."

He felt a burst of anger shoot through him. Those birds down at the other end of the counter had no business getting into his business. He felt his thigh muscles knot as he clamped his legs around the stool. He looked back at the waitress, who was still grinning, and found himself grinning back. "That's who I am, I guess," he admitted with a shrug.

"Well, don't let it hold your appetite back. Pitch in," she said.

"All right."

"And drink your milk."

He nodded, and reached toward it.

"This your first time in town?" she asked.

"That's right. Ten-hour pass."

"I heard you don't get off the post much."

He shot a look down to the other end of the counter.

111

"Relax, Killer. They didn't give me your biography. They didn't have to. We get soldiers in here every night. You're a pretty steady subject of conversation."

He grunted, thinking that over. It was the first time he'd had any idea of that. He wondered just what she'd heard.

"Go on, try the steak. It won't kill you," she said. She looked past him, saw new customers coming in, and muttered something under her breath as she moved off to serve them. She turned her head back long enough to say "My name's Maggie Banks, by the way," and then Sullivan was left alone with his steak.

He had no other place to go, that he could think of, so he stayed in the lunch room, occasionally drinking another glass of milk, and talking to Maggie for a few minutes every once in a while.

"I hear you're from Earth."

He bridled a little. "That's right. I'm a Mole."

"Relax. If there's Venusian Plutonians, I guess there's room for you, too. You signed a contract with the Settler's Council. That's all the citizenship papers you need."

"Some people don't think so."

"There's some of those in every crowd."

A little later he asked her what living on Pluto had been like.

"Pretty miserable," she answered. "My dad had a farm out near the dam. I hear they're finishing it up now, to get the power, but when I was out there we had floods more often than not. Finally washed us out. Dad got a job in one of the Settler's Council's first big projects—cooperative farm, with a freezer plant so the surplus could be stockpiled for when they had to pull the labor off the farms and into the factories. He fell into a disker. Mom was in a factory, truing bedplates. I got this job a couple of years ago, when everybody moved into town.

Mom died a year ago last month. Too much metal dust in her lungs. I'm twenty-eight, healthy and unmarried. Now—what's *your* story?"

He'd never had to tell one before, and did a poor job of it. She stopped him in the middle of it.

"Killer, you're a clumsy man with a lie. Suppose we take a rain-check on it and you tell me sometime later, when you've had a chance to polish it up."

He grinned sheepishly, and she laughed.

And finally she said:

"Well, Killer, it's closing time. You look like a big, strong man. Care to see a helpless lady home?"

"All right."

He paid his check, and the two of them walked through the town to her dormitory. He didn't have much to say, and neither did she, except to ask, once:

"Sullivan, what's your first name?"

He told her, and she let it go at that for the time being. When they reached the entrance to the dormitory, she shook his hand and said "Thanks for taking me home, Jack. Be seeing you," and went in.

He walked slowly back to the post, reported in, and lay down for an hour before reveille, looking up at the ceiling in the dark, turning "Be seeing you" over in his mind.

He stayed preoccupied through the day, feeling a peculiar restlessness and a dull lack of interest in anything going on around him. He discovered he couldn't remember what Maggie looked like, and he frowned over the problem for hours, trying to build up an image in his mind, but his visual memory was completely obscured by long passages of totally recalled conversation—the sound of her voice when she said "Be seeing you" insisted on getting in his way. He knew he'd recognize her the minute he saw her—he had absolutely no doubt

113

of that—but meanwhile, without a picture of her in his memory, he felt as though there was something missing . . . something he ought to have, but didn't. He was vaguely irritated, and vaguely upset. At one point Kovacs asked him, "What's the matter today, Sullivan? Off your feed?" Sullivan looked at him quickly and closely, but he finally decided that Kovacs had just been using his sharp instruction field voice through habit and had just happened to pull the expression out of thin air. He shook his head and said "No, sir," and Kovacs slapped his back, saying, "All right, Killer, now let's show the rest of these birds how to fight house-to-house," and that had been that.

Toward the end of the day, Hungerford had looked at him with a slow grin and said "Killer, you must have found something in town last night."

Sullivan, startled, looked at him in panic. Then he realized it probably didn't take much guessing, and that, besides, Hungerford wasn't likely to be giving him away to anyone. He felt embarrassed, and just grinned back. Then another thought struck him, and he wondered how he'd managed to forget the most important detail.

"I'd like to have another pass tonight," he said, and was both surprised and angry when Hungerford shook his head.

"Sorry, but I can't do it. You're supposed to sleep sometime, you know. The best I can do is to promise you one for tomorrow."

Tomorrow was too far away. He started to say something, but Hungerford cut him off.

"No pass tonight, and no arguments. This is still an army. I can stretch the regulations some, but not that much."

So Sullivan spent the time between evening chow and lights out in various torturesome ways, banging his knife into the board until Hungerford came out and pulled the board down, and then hanging around the fringes of a crap game, and finally simply lying on his bunk and trying to shut his mind off so he could get some sleep. The following day was just as bad—worse; tempered by impatience—and he took his shower after chow with a racking mixture of haste and painstaking care.

He'd started earlier today, so he got into Port Mac-Donnel while it was still light. He walked quickly through the town and to the lunch room. He went inside and stood just beyond the door, watching Maggie straightening out a place at the counter and putting dirty dishes in the washer. When she looked up, saw him and grinned, he grinned back in relief. She was just exactly the way he remembered her. He walked awkwardly up to the counter, painfully self-conscious, and sat down.

"Hi, Maggie."

"Hello, Jack. Got yourself another pass, huh?"

"That's right," he said, and then realized it was at least six hours to closing time.

So, while Maggie waited on customers and talked to him for short times in between, he sat his way through it, feeling better now that he was back in the lunch room, and feeling impatient for some privacy.

"Tell me something, Jack," she said at one point, "I heard a lot of stuff about you. You're supposed to be a pretty rough customer. Mean. That true?"

He shrugged. He didn't much want to talk about it.

"Damned if *I* can see it," she said.

"Maybe I don't act my usual way around you."

"Maybe you don't. You look big enough. Ever done any farming?"

He shook his head.

"Ever thought about it? Whatcha planning on doing with your land?"

He grinned crookedly, looking down at his hands on the counter. "I used to figure I'd build a house on it. Farm it, maybe."

"You used to, huh? What happened?"

"Well," he said uncomfortably, "things happen to make a man change his mind. Tell you the truth, I don't think about it much."

"Well, a man can think again, I guess," she said, moving away.

After a while she had a chance to come back. She leaned on the counter. "I've been thinking," she said. "You're no more'n thirty-five, right? Time you get out, you'll only be forty. A man like you, healthy, knows how to take care of himself—man like that's not anywheres near too old to start a place. Look—pretty soon, you'll get made a non-com corporal for sure, and maybe a sergeant. All you boys that're in now'll get made non-coms pretty soon, so you can train the men that'll be free when the factories start running automated. So you can figure on maybe a hundred and seventy-five or two hundred acres comin' to you by the time you muster out. 'Course, that land isn't too hot, but you can sell it and maybe get ninety acres of prime land. That'll take good care of a family."

He looked at her and grinned, feeling a little short-winded. "You've been figuring, eh? Know all about what the army's gonna do."

She looked back at him frankly. "Sure, I've been figuring. No harm in it. And why shouldn't I know about the way the army's set up? Everybody else does. Heck, *you're* in it—don't you ever think about getting your promotion?"

He shook his head. "Why should I? I've got enough to worry about, just being a good soldier and learning

116

how to take care of myself," he said cautiously. He didn't want to tell her, yet, about the plans Kovacs had for him. There'd be time enough for that when it worked out. And now, for the first time, he was thinking beyond the war. He realized for the first time that there must inevitably be a day when there would be no more fighting for him. And yet, he would have to be doing *something*. Time would not stop with the end of the war.

It was an astonishing revelation.

Sullivan had fallen out of the practice of paying attention to things that weren't his business. It kept things simpler all around.

But now, he thought, while Maggie had to leave him and get back to work again, now things were a little different.

Buy a farm. It sounded good. Build your own house, live on your own land, eating food you grew yourself —raise kids. And on an officer's land grant—not a non-com's.

He sat with his folded hands under his chin, staring into space and thinking. Maggie'd guessed him to be thirty-five. He would have said he looked a little younger, himself. Maybe he didn't look as closely at himself as she did. Anyway—his fiftieth birthday was due in a few weeks. That was by the calendar. How old was he, really, though? He wished he knew whether age was something purely physical or whether there was more to it than that. He knew how old he looked, and he knew how old he felt. He could think in terms of a future that stretched out for years to come. Maybe he was wrong. At the end of threescore years and ten, or however much had been allotted to him, he might simply wither away and die, and leave his wife and kids without a man. He wondered whether he could even have children.

117

But it was better to be wrong and take the chance, than to be wrong in the other direction and die, some day, as a lonely and extraordinarily old man thinking of what he might have had.

He saw Maggie coming back to him again, and it wasn't just the lonely soldier in him who felt the smile growing at the corners of his mouth, but the whole uncertain, battered man.

He walked her home again, both of them walking more slowly this time.

"Jack, you're a funny guy. There's more to you than I heard, and more'n you tell me, too. That's all right; there's plenty of men around you can find out the whole of in no more time'n it takes to mention the weather. What counts is, you can take care of yourself and some to spare for the people with you, if you want to. You're a good soldier—you're maybe the best in the army, right now, and don't think the guys I hear talkin' in the lunch room don't know it. It annoys them some." She grinned up at him, for a moment, and then went back to being serious. "It's a rough life out in the back country, even nowadays. It takes a good man to keep his land under him when the storms hit or the winter nails you down. You done any more thinkin' about that farm?"

He nodded. "Sounds like a pretty good idea. I think I'd like it."

She nodded, too, and they walked along. As they came near her dormitory, she said, "You know, opinion's kind of divided about you. Only one thing about it's what you might call flattery; there isn't a man in the army that doesn't look over his shoulder just to make sure before he starts talking about what an ape you are. Some say you're crazy and some say you're stupid. Some say both. But I wanted to get a look at you for myself. All right, so I'll tell you what I think. You're a big man and you're complicated inside. I think maybe there's more to all that than meets the eye. From what I've seen of you, you'll do. I'd like to see more of you. You can please yourself about that, and about whatever you think of me. Now I've said what I figure I ought to get on the books, and any time you want to add your share to it, that's up to you."

"All right," he said, keeping his voice deliberate. He felt something welling up inside him, driving out the cold. "I'll be seeing you pretty often, I guess."

"A'l right."

He walked her to her door, and they stood motionless under the small light, with the sprawled wooden building looming beside them. Sullivan looked at Maggie hesitantly. He felt something cold gather in the pit of his stomach. Then he broke through his paralysis with an abrupt step forward, and kissed her good night after all.

XIII

"UP TO NOW," Kovacs said at roster a few days later, "you men have been going through a training program designed to make good soldiers out of you. And those of you who're still here are good soldiers. One or two of you are the best there is. We've toughened you up and knocked the lumps off you. We've been on your backs all day, every day, weeding the congenital weaklings out of this platoon and leaving nothing but the men. And I suppose those of you here feel pretty good about it."

Sullivan shifted his feet a little restlessly. He was

thinking about the pass waiting for him in Hungerford's office tonight.

"So," Kovacs said in a falsely casual voice, "you won't think anything of it when I tell you the next few weeks are going to cut this platoon down by one-third. And I mean every man of that. We're moving the schedule up. If you thought you were getting it tough before, now you'll think we've wrapped bobwire around it. A number of you are going to die. You will all train harder, soldier better, and do it faster. You men are not training to get yourselves killed or mess things up the first time you go into action. You are training to *lead*, and you *will* lead, and you will lead *smart!* You are training to *train*, and by God there won't be *anything* you don't know so well you couldn't teach it to a blind man with his ears plugged up. We don't have any combat veterans in this army. Well, by the time I get through with you, those of you still on top of the ground will be able to say you fought Kovacs' War! This is going to be the best platoon in the whole army! The best platoon in the best company in the best army there is! And when this platoon gets broken up and you men get recruit squads of your own, the commanding general is by God going to be able to tell at a glance which of his non-coms came out of Kovacs' platoon!

"All right, now we've got that straight, you can take over, Hungerford."

Hungerford stepped forward. Sullivan noticed he was a little red-eyed this morning, and a little pale. He guessed the liquor was beginning to catch up with the sergeant, and he growled a little, deep in his throat. Hungerford was too good a man for that kind of thing.

He noticed, too, that the men in the platoon weren't reacting very much to Kovacs' speech. Saddler hadn't even grunted. The word must have been around on the grapevine already. He twitched his mouth as he

120

realized it could have been on the grapevine for weeks without his hearing it.

"You heard the lieutenant," Hungerford said in a blurred voice. "Today we're hooked up with a chemical warfare combat team. You're going to be issued new equipment on the field, and you'll get instructions on it. Then you're going to go out on the field and use it. You better learn quick, because the CW boys won't be pulling their punches. You'll get all this in detail later, from the specialists. After chow, you will fall in here, with your battle armor on. All right, you're dismissed. Go get something in your stomachs." He turned listlessly away, and had to set his feet carefully. Kovacs couldn't have helped noticing—Sullivan saw him look directly at Hungerford—but he did nothing. Sullivan wondered why, and what was wrong with the sergeant.

He smiled to himself a little, and at himself, as well. He was changing. A few weeks ago Hungerford's troubles would have been Hungerford's troubles, and Sullivan wouldn't have cared.

No—he might have cared some, in Hungerford's case. Even then, he wouldn't have wasted much time thinking about it.

Sullivan thought about Maggie as he sat down. She'd really started something turning over in him, and his old way of looking at things was going to pieces. He looked around him, conscious of the careful clear space the other men at the table kept around him, and the dead silence among them, and something in his throat began to ache.

He went back to the barracks after chow and got into his armor, still moody, and when the platoon formed up he stood next to Saddler and wonder what the other man would do if he said something to him.

He walked slowly into the lunch room, his hands

121

shivering, and dropped down on the farthest stool. He looked around to see if there were any other soldiers in the place, and when he saw there weren't, he let himself go and leaned on his elbows, covering his eyes with the heels of his hands. He kept his teeth clenched, and his breath hissed raggedly through him.

Maggie had stared at the look on his face when he came in. She got down to his end of the counter.

"What's the matter, Jack?"

Sullivan shook his head. "Fellow in the platoon got killed today. We got issued a kind of filter that clips onto your battle helmet. Supposed to seal it up tight, and pass the air you breathe through some kind of complicated gizmo. Supposed to take out any germs or poisons. Well, we got checked out on the things, and then we got some stuff fired at us by the chemical warfare boys. Antipersonnel gas of some kind. Doesn't matter which one, the procedure's the same. You start your filter and keep going through it. Something went wrong with the gizmo in this fellow's filter. The stuff got through. This fellow Saddler went down and started screaming, with his radio circuit on, of course. We couldn't even hold him still long enough to switch it off. After a while—not very long—he was making sounds like nothing I ever heard. The CW boys said the stuff was taking out his lungs and throat. The whole business lasted about a minute."

Maggie's hand twitched on his arm. After a minute she asked: "This Saddler fellow—he *couldn't* have been a friend of yours, could he?"

Sullivan shook his head. "I don't know if he could or not."

.

He went doggedly through the next few days, forming up for roster next to a man named Root, but he paid very little attention to what was going on around

122

him. The platoon lost more men. The ferocity of the training impressed itself on him only by shrinking the ranks in which he formed up each morning, stone-faced and with eyes that peered redly from behind crusted lashes. There were no more replacements being funneled in. The cadre was set, and Sullivan wondered how much longer it was going to be before the orders came down and they were broken up to staff the new training plant being built next to the old area. The builders were at it night and day, and some of the new barracks were already finished.

Hungerford was still giving him passes into town every other day, signing them in a shaky hand. Sullivan tried to find out what the sergeant's trouble was. But Hungerford had stopped talking almost completely. The one time Sullivan tried to ask him, Hungerford looked up with a loose, crooked twist in his face, his hair falling down on his forehead, and swept his arm in a pawing gesture that took in all of the post. "This," he said, and lapsed back into looking at the print on the opposite wall.

And that was the best Sullivan could do.

But it was all coming to a head. Sullivan knew it whenever he walked up Port MacDonnel's main street toward Maggie. The town was alive with it. There were many more people out nights than usual, and they were stirring with some kind of excitement. While he and the platoon maneuvered through radioactive barrages, or fought to train their missile launchers on tanks whining out of clouds of fire, the new factories in Port Mac-Donnel had been going into their first production one by one. The glare of welding torches had disappeared from behind the windows and been replaced by work lights. The whine of cranes and power hoists moving automatic machinery into place had ended, and now he heard the steady rumble of work moving along the

123

lines. There were still a few work teams going through the old factories left over from the colony, bringing them up to the new standard, and when they were through—maybe they *were* through—Port MacDonnel's industries would start delivering their product.

The whole business—the whole tightly organized program—was just about ready to go into its last stage.

And John L. Sullivan, his big, muscle-sheathed body as numb as his thought processes, realized clearly that he no longer cared about the purpose of his training or the Settlers' Council's plans. He had been shaped and worked into a perfect fighting man. When the time came, he would do what he was told. If he was told to give orders, he would give the best possible orders, and see to it that his men did whatever was necessary. But he did not think about himself in relation to Pluto's future, or Earth's. He had even forgotten the occasional daydream of some day breaking into Mr. Small's office with a Bofors in his hand.

The night came when he was walking down the company street, on his way back from Maggie's. Kovacs, on the day room steps, called his name sharply. He jerked his head up, coming a little way out of his shell.

"Killer! I was just looking for you. Hungerford said you were out on a pass."

"Yes, sir."

"Well, I'm glad you're back, anyway. I've got good news for you. I've had some myself." Kovacs' eyes were glittering. "I'm Acting Major Kovacs now!"

"Congratulations, sir," Sullivan said dully.

"The orders just came down. Everybody's jumping grades. You're going to be a corporal in Hungerford's new platoon." Kovacs touched his arm. "After the training cycle, that'll be a lieutenant's commission."

"Yes, sir." Sullivan shrugged in the darkness of the street.

"The first batch of recruits arrives in the new training facilities day after tomorrow. The expansion's on. Everybody in this company's a non-com now. We're on our way, Killer!"

"That's very good, sir."

"Yes," Kovacs whispered in the night. "That's perfect."

XIV

June, 2198, on Earth and on Pluto where the flaming satellite circled the planet once in twenty-four hours and the planetary year was too long to count. The final training cycle was nearly over.

On the spacefield at Port MacDonnel, Corporal John L. Sullivan sent a look along the ranks of his and Hungerford's platoon. They stood at parade rest, rifle butts beside their boots, barrels all tilted at the identical angle, hands gripping the polished steel all in exactly the same place.

They were perfectly trained. He and Hungerford had taken these farmers-turned-mill hands, these lean and starve-faced sons of Interplanetary Resources' abandoned people, had molded these mill hands-turned-soldiers into precision machines. They had ground them down and killed and toughened them, and Sullivan knew—everyone knew—there was nothing on Earth that could stand up to them. He and Hungerford had done that. He mechanically, not caring and yet doing a perfect job because he was himself a perfect soldier, and Hungerford drunkenly.

He looked at Hungerford, standing two paces in front of the ranked platoon. He was as bad as Sullivan had ever seen him. The man's face was streaming with cold perspiration. His skin was doughy. Sullivan could see the men sneaking looks at him, wondering if he was going to keep his feet.

Sullivan sighed. Hungerford always did. You had to give him that. He had yet to make a public disgrace of himself. But Kovacs knew the man was always in a stupor. Plenty of the other regimental officers knew it. And still, nothing was done about it. In the perfect army, Hungerford was a tolerated rotten spot. Why?

Sullivan growled a little to himself. He had given up trying to get through to the man. They barely spoke to each other outside their duties. Hungerford gave him his passes, his signature scrawled at the bottom, and that was all.

Sullivan noticed that Barker, the second man from the end of the rank, had been careless again. There was a smudge on his helmet visor. He sent Barker one of his special looks, and the man blanched.

It was an odd feeling. Barker was a big, tough man. Simply by looking at him, Sullivan had made his belly contract in fear. And yet Sullivan himself felt nothing—no rancor, no special thing of any kind. It was automatic. A man slipped, and you made sure he wouldn't do it again. Not because it mattered a damn if one man in an honor guard of a hundred had a fingermark on one corner of his visor, but because a careless man could not be allowed to keep that luxurious trait in an army that was going to march against a world. And yet this had nothing to do with any wish on Sullivan's part to be a conqueror. It had to do only with his being a corporal—with his going to be a lieutenant.

That was the trick. Keep it simple, and you got through the day. It didn't matter that only Kovacs spoke to you off duty, and that only Hungerford, still, occasionally acted as though you were human. You got through the day, and then you got your pass and went to sit in the diner until it was time to walk Maggie home.

He and Maggie didn't even talk much, these days. There was no need. They had decided what little of their future was allowed them for deciding, and now there was nothing to do but wait for the end of the war. They spoke in brief sentences, walked slowly to her dormitory, kissed and parted. They were caught up in the immovable working-out of the Settlers' Councils' plans, and there was no way to break free. Neither of them spoke of it. But they felt it, day and night, and did not even think that they had any right to expect anything different.

The cold wind numbed Sullivan's face. The hard light of Pluto's sun lanced from the gleaming hulls of the heavy spaceships that towered on the field. There was a steady undercurrent of motor noises and cargo winches. Tons of crated equipment were being taken aboard the ships in a constant operation that did not stop for the imminent arrival of one ship, or for its honor guard.

"Attention." The command crackled in over their helmet receivers. The ranks brought their heels together in a massed clack. Shoulders straightened. Heads came up. A silver flash grew in the sky.

The ship came down, and Sullivan noticed, without using the fact for a datum, that the ship was not built in one of Pluto's yards. It was too small, and too graceful.

"Present . . . arms."

The rifle barrels flashed in the sun. A closed car rolled up to the ship. A door opened in the ship's hull. Someone came out, too far away from Sullivan to be recognized, and got in the car. The car rolled off the field and went in the direction of the Settlers' Council office building, a rough gray concrete pile at the edge of Port MacDonnel.

"Platoon sergeants will form their men and march them back to the military area."

The honor guard was dismissed from duty. Someone important had come to Pluto, but Sullivan made nothing of it. He had been ordered to form part of an honor guard, and he had done so. Now there were other duties.

Hungerford dismissed the platoon for mess, once they were back at the barracks and out of their dress uniforms. "Not you, Barker," Sullivan said casually, and the man, who'd known better than to move off with the rest of the platoon, looked at him with terrible expectancy. Sullivan walked over and lifted the helmet out of Barker's locker. "Put it on."

Barker dropped the helmet down over his head. Sullivan closed the visor over his face. Taking a piece of wire out of his pocket, Sullivan tied down the visor locks so it couldn't be raised again.

"Twenty-four hours, Barker." There was no point in reminding the man what would happen to him if he was seen with the helmet off during that time. "And you won't do it again, will you?"

"No, corporal." Barker's voice was muffled inside the helmet. He could breathe, and see out, and hear. But he could not eat, or wipe the perspiration off his face, or scratch his itching scalp. In a few hours, the helmet would become intolerable.

"That's all."

Barker saluted.

And that was that. That was the army way, and Sullivan was an army man.

Barker was free to do what he liked while the remainder of the platoon was at mess. So was Sullivan, who didn't feel much like eating. Barker went into the latrine. Sullivan stretched out on his bunk, cupped his hands behind his head, and stared up without thinking.

Someone came into the barracks from the day room.

"Corporal?"

Sullivan rolled over on his side and grunted. "Yeah?"

"Sergeant Hungerford wants to see you."

So Hungerford hadn't gone to eat, either. It wasn't particularly surprising. But what did he want Sullivan for?

Sullivan sighed, dropped his booted feet back down to the floor and stood up. He walked across the barracks to the day room door, slammed it shut behind him, and stopped in Hungerford's office doorway. "Yeah?"

Hungerford looked up from behind his desk, nodded at a chair, and motioned Sullivan inside. "Have a seat."

Sullivan lowered himself into the chair. Hungerford's shirt was half out of the tops of his pants. His sleeves had been rolled up, but they'd slipped back down his forearms and the cuffs were flapping at his wrists. There was a half-empty bottle sitting on the corner of the desk.

"Just like old times," he said, catching Sullivan's glance at the bottle. "I send for Killer Sullivan and in he comes and looks at me contemptuously. Him, of all people."

Sullivan looked at him coldly. "I used to stand up. Now I sit." He let the rest of it go. You don't bother pushing guys that're going downhill already.

Hungerford's eyebrow went up. "Oh, things change, all right, Sullivan. But somehow they're just like old times anyway."

Sullivan grimaced.

Hungerford lifted his bottle, took a pull on it, and set it down. He looked at Sullivan. "That's none of your business."

"All right. Stop feeling guilty about it. I don't care what you do. But the men ain't going to go on much

129

longer without blabbing it around where some officer's going to hear it. I don't think your rep's in good enough shape any more to stand up to a knock like that."

Hungerford twitched his shoulders. "So? Is there an easier way for you to make sergeant?"

Sullivan kept his mouth shut.

Hungerford straightened his head with a jerk. "I want someone to talk to."

"Me?"

"Why not?" Hungerford looked at the Feurmann print he'd moved to this new barracks from the old, and put up where he could stare at it. "Ship," he said. "Rocket ship. Not like the one that came down today. Noisy, blundering old rocket ship. Couldn't get to that star it's aiming for if it had a hundred years. But that *MacDonnel* powered ship, now . . . That's a different story, eh, Sullivan?"

"I wouldn't know."

"No. No, you wouldn't. Nobody would. Oh, a few people, here and there. But not the average man. Not even the above-average man. Wears his MacDonnel belt to commute in, floats around in his MacDonnel runabout come weekends . . . but who wants to *go* anywhere? Who wants to give up living on the fat of the next generation? How long'd it take you to get across the Solar System when you came here from Earth, Sullivan? A week? Do you *know*—can you *imagine*—how long it would take you in a *rocket?*" Hungerford laughed. "And that was in a beat-up old freighter, with a unit that was maybe ten percent efficient. You take one of the new MacDonnels—one of the hundred per cent efficient jobs, like that ship had that came down today—you know what you can do with one of those? You can beat *Einstein*—Albert Einstein, the man who slammed the gate on the stars. Because it *isn't* anti*gravity*, of course. This isn't Cavorite we're using. It's anti-*mass*.

130

But you don't know H. G. Wells. Writer. Romancer. *But it can be done!*" Hungerford's fist came down on the desk. "It can be *done!* Mass can be nullified, and a flick of a spitball out the stern ports can send a million cubic feet of hull to Andromeda, and in a twinkling. If. If. If, *if* anyone wants to go!"

Sullivan felt his face twist in disgust as tears began to run down Hungerford's cheeks.

Hungerrord rolled back in his chair. "Big, rough-tough Killer Sullivan. Runs the barracks with an iron hand. Ought to make captain, anyway, during the war. Figuring on it. Am I right? I thought so." He grinned loosely and raised the bottle again. "Sullivan, I toast you. To the green youth who came stumbling out here from Earth, and turned to stone. What happened to bring you out here, Sullivan or whatever your name is?"

Sullivan looked at him.

"It takes one to call one, Killer," Hungerford said. "No history, no luggage, and no name. That's not you —it's me, walking up to the man at the constabulary recruiting desk and signing my mother's maiden name. That was before we were so well organized out here, or I couldn't have made it. I wonder if anybody's ever curious about what happened to me. Do you? Wonder about you, I mean?"

Sullivan looked at Hungerford and began to see a few things. He shrugged. "Nobody I know back there has the time to waste, wondering."

"I'm glad to see we're approaching a communion of souls," Hungerford smiled. "Brothers under the skin. So what good did it do us? Did we get away from anything? No. We just trapped ourselves. You—I don't know. You've got something on your back, stuck tight. I don't know what it is, but I can see what it's doing to you. For myself, what's going to happen to me is pretty obvious. And both of us have turned into something we might not like so much if we met it as we were."

"You're wrong."

"*You're* wrong. The advantage of alcohol is that occasionally you sober up and have a chance to observe your progress."

Hungerford laughed. "We think the outside is the man. The uniform; the mannerisms; the new name. We lie down on Doncaster's table, and push the old man away. We let the other man come out—the opposite, the other part—or is he only one of many?—*out* he comes, up to the surface, and we think we have liberated ourselves. But *what have we done?* Have we killed the other man? Have we wiped him out? Oh, no—no, no, for he is still of us." Hungerford tapped his skull. "Somewhere in there—somewhere in here—he hides, he lurks, and now *he* is trapped and now *he* wants to get out, and now *he* makes us hate ourselves for what we are. And did you think of that, Sullivan? Did they think of that, at Doncaster, before they conspired with you to rob that man and hurl him into darkness? Did you? Never! You did not think, I did not think, and somewhere in here, now, there's a man called Angus Mac-Donnel who screams that he can't live with Sergeant Hungerford. He's a man who remembers his grandfather, and the wonderful gimmick that was going to take us all out to the stars. His grandfather, dying of cancer, eating himself up because he was rich from MacDonnel runabouts and MacDonnel commuter belts, and because no one wanted anything but a better runabout, with bigger back seats for their fat wives to sit in on a Sunday's trip to Aunt Susie's house, and better belts so they'd get to the office faster.

"And my father, living off the estate, sitting and enjoying it, loving it—loving not having to work, or dream; *glad* he took after the maternal side of the family.

132

And me. *Me!* Me, and the thing I'm doing. Me, that not even Kovacs dares to touch.

"So, tell me, Sullivan—who's inside you that hates your guts? Who screams and hammers inside your head?"

XV

THE ARMY did not go out to the training ground that afternoon. Just as the last men were reporting back from mess, the base public address system came to life.

There was a crackle and a sputter from the loudspeaker in Sullivan's barracks. "Attention!" the cold voice said. "All scheduled exercises are suspended. Condition Able is effective immediately. Repeat . . ."

Sullivan sat up from where he'd been brooding on the edge of his bunk. His voice drowned out the loudspeaker.

"All right, you men! Fall in on the company street in twenty minutes. You will be in battle dress. You will have your gear packed. You will have drawn your rifles from the orderly room corporal. You will be ready in all respects to move out. You will have stripped your bunks. You will have packed or abandoned all personal effects. Twenty minutes. Go!"

The orders came automatically. Condition Able was the code phrase in which all the noncommissioned officers had long ago been instructed. What it meant was that today was the day, and it had triggered Sullivan's response as cleanly as an electric current applied to a frog's nerve.

But Sullivan was only part frog. In the sudden tumult of the barracks, he was changing uniforms and packing his gear as quickly and efficiently as anyone, but he was

133

barely paying attention to what he was doing. Once, he stopped and shouted: "Barker—you can unglue that helmet." But that, too, was automatic.

He was listening. With great intensity, he was listening for a voice in his head.

He wondered if Hungerford would make it to the formation. Sullivan had got out of the sergeant's office as quickly as he could, without speaking, and Hungerford had been slumped across the desk. He wondered. But, without interruption, most of all, he listened.

He formed up his platoon on the company street. They stood at rest, their duffel bags beside them, their packs on their backs and their rifles in their hands. Sullivan faced them, and Hungerford had not come out of the barracks. Sullivan wondered if he should have gone in there and got him. But what possible use could it be? The best thing for Hungerford was for him to stay exactly where he was. The army would go, and Hungerford would be free to slip into his glass womb.

So Hungerford was Donel MacDonnel's grandson. Sullivan remembered his picture in the newspapers—a burly, broken-nosed man with stiff blond hair and a fanatic's ice blue eyes, and a long record of arrests for civil disobedience. He had drifted out of the public's eye at last, and anyone who thought of it was certainly glad to see the rabble-rouser go, with his speeches and lunatic-fringe demonstrations in front of government offices. And so here he was now. And so Doncaster had made a practice of using Pluto for a dumping-ground.

Kovacs came hurrying around the corner of the barracks, frowning when he saw that Sullivan was alone.

"Where's Hungerford?" He had been elated by the marching orders. His voice was deadly in its betrayal of his sudden anger.

Sullivan looked him in the eyes. "I'm sorry, sir. I
134

don't know. I haven't seen him since mess call." Kovacs was in his battle uniform, his officer's helmet thrown back and locked behind his head, his Bofors glistening at his belt. He looked speculatively at Sullivan. "You don't know." He pursed his lips. "Why didn't you report him missing?"

"There was no reason to, sir. Not until Condition Able was announced. And then my primary duty was to get the platoon into formation."

Kovacs clicked his tongue sharply. "Yes. Of course. And what do you propose we do now? Hold up the war for him? The entire company is in formation and ready. Corporal, I—*By Heaven, if he's not out here in marching uniform in two minutes, I'll have him shot for desertion. On the spot. Friends high up or no friends high up.* Go get him, Sullivan. If you want to be a lieutenant."

Sullivan had put himself at rigid attention. He held that posture, because it let him keep his face blank.

Kovacs had raised a question with his last order, though he could not have had any idea of that, or of its effect on Sullivan.

"Well, corporal, are we holding up the war for you, too?" The major's insignia glittered on Kovacs' shoulders.

Then Hungerford came lurching out of the barracks, still dressed in his shapeless fatigues. He held the nearly empty bottle in his hand.

Sullivan snapped around toward the platoon. "'Tenshun!" he roared. "Eyes *front!*" That smashed down the mutter that had risen among the men. But it did nothing to stop Kovacs. The officer charged toward Hungerford, who was standing on the day room steps with a rigid arm braced on the handrail.

A car was rolling down the company street.

Kovacs reached Hungerford. His hand clawed out and

135

dragged the sergeant stumbling down. Hungerford some-how kept his feet. He looked at Kovacs without any expression, and did not seem to notice the officer's clutch at his forearm. Kovacs's hand was clawed, the nails digging in. His lips were glazed with moisture. He had not yet said a word, but thin, high, tortured sounds escaped him faintly, as though his throat had locked.

Sullivan had no idea of what to do. Hungerford's head was bent, now, and his face was only inches away from Kovacs'. His eyes looked bottomlessly into the officer's, and his face was smeared where he had at some point rubbed away the tears.

The car reached a point abreast of the platoon and stopped. A man in civilian clothes got out of the back. He was enormously fat, with great jowls rolling over his collar. His long, curly black hair hung from the sides of his bald scalp and covered the tops of his ears. His nose was deeply furrowed across the bridge, where something hard and thin had once cut into it with brutal force.

His almost invisible eyes flickered from Kovacs and Hungerford, over the rigid platoon, to Sullivan. "Call attention," he said in a voice that had been damaged by the injury to his nose.

The sound of Sullivan's voice froze Kovacs. Hunger-ford looked out over his shoulder, saw the obese man, and said to him: "You're late."

The civilian seemed unable to raise his voice above its harsh quietness. "Don't be arrogant. There is no purpose in abusing one's high value, once one has it." Then he said: "But, I apologize. I am here now."

Kovacs turned around. "Mister Councilman."

The civilian frowned at him. "I don't know you . . ." His eyes touched on Kovacs' insignia. "Major."

136

Kovacs was silent. The civilian looked back to Hungerford. "Where's your man?"

Hungerford pointed. "Him."

"The corporal? Yes. I've seen you on the street, Sullivan, without knowing who you were. I remember you impressed me.

"Major, you will detail two temporary noncommissioned officers for this platoon. Hungerford and Sullivan are coming with me."

"Yes, sir," Kovacs said.

Hungerford swayed toward the car. The civilian looked at him, and took the bottle out of his hand as he went by. He dropped it on the ground and stepped on it. The glass splintered with a sharp crack. The whiskey formed a puddle around the man's slippered foot.

Hungerford paid no attention. He stopped in the car's doorway. "Come *on*, Killer," he said peevishly before he climbed in.

Sullivan picked up his gear and got into the back seat with it. The civilian squeezed in beside him. He signaled to the chauffeur. The door closed and they rolled away. Sullivan turned his head and looked back at Major Kovacs, standing there.

They stopped in front of the Settlers' Council office building. The civilian pushed himself out. "You can leave your gear in the car," he said to Sullivan. "It'll be taken care of. I suggest you leave your helmet and rifle, as well. You may certainly keep your sidearm, if you wish."

Sullivan followed orders without speaking. He and Hungerford went up the steps with the civilian as the car pulled away. Sullivan noticed that Hungerford's mouth was set in a desperate line, as though something he loathed were waiting for him inside the building.

But Sullivan was not wondering what might be waiting

there for himself, or why he was here. As he walked up the steps; as he and Hungerford followed the obese man through narrow corridors lit only by a single bulb here and there; as they made their way past armed civilian guards with the impersonally merciless look of the immigration clerks at the spacefield; still, and not caring really what went on about him, Sullivan was listening.

"We go in here," the civilian said, and opened an unmarked door. He opened it wide, and Sullivan, coming in after him, saw a large room with a curtained window. The walls were banked with old wooden filing cabinets, their drawers dated and marked "Plan Fulfillment Reports." The earliest date was a century ago, and the smell of old paper filled the room.

There were a dozen men in it. All of them, in one way or another, were very much like the man who had brought them, even though some were thin, some tall, some short, and one was Mr. Small. They sat in arm-chairs behind a long table, and the obese man sank gratefully into his own place.

Hungerford and Sullivan stood facing them. Mr. Small said:

"How do you do? These gentleman beside me are the Plutonian Settlers' Council, as I may assume you've gathered. And you are, of course, Angus MacDonnel and Allen Sibley. I am pleased to see you again, though Mr. MacDonnel does not look very fit."

Hungerford made a spitting noise. "My condition hasn't ever been of much concern to you. Nor did it keep me from giving you John L. Sullivan as he is today —precisely the man you need. You'll pardon my minor vices in exchange."

Small's eyebrows arched. "Of course, Mr. MacDonnel. I was only remarking." He sat behind his desk, much the same as ever, and was invulnerable. He turned to

Sullivan. "I'm gratified to see you in an excellent physical state, Mr. Sibley. And with quite an enviable reputation. May I congratulate you on your success with yourself?"

A growl rumbled up in Sullivan's throat. "It was you on that ship today."

Small nodded. "Of course. The Settlers' Council is our most important corporate subsidiary. It was essential that I be here on this crucial day."

"And what do you need me for?"

Hungerford answered. "They need a leader. Somebody like you, Killer. Somebody dynamic. Somebody with drive, and toughness; and brains, under that shell."

Small nodded. "That's true in a way. Though I would not have you think you were hand-picked from the start. Doncaster would hardly put all its eggs in one basket. We are too old, too large, Mr. Sibley, to take such a risk as that. Corporate management, as you know, must involve many safeguards and alternative means to the ultimate end. I would not have you think that, in an otherwise carefully weighed program, Doncaster would make such an error." This seemed to be quite important to Small. He peered at Sullivan, impressing his point. "It happens that you are the best candidate we have developed for a post which Doncaster foresaw, years ago, would have to be filled today. I trust—I am confident—that I and my predecessors did not err in our evaluation, and that you, indeed fulfilling Doncaster's genuine need, will not fail us."

John L. Sullivan looked at Small, and felt something wrench open inside him. "You're wrong," he said. "You're dead wrong. I'm quitting the army. I've had it. I don't want your goddam officer's commission. I don't want anything. I don't want to go fight a war on Earth. I'm *through*." Now, he thought. Now are you satisfied, Sibley? Will you leave me alone?

Small touched his teeth to his lip. "I see," he said quietly. "Mr. Sibley, let me explain something in greater detail. I must ask you to consider Doncaster's corporate position. I must ask you to consider the economic course of Earth." He put up a quick thin hand. "Please, Mr. Sibley. Bear with me."

Sullivan looked around the Council. They were gazing back at him dispassionately, and all the while each of their chairs was turned slightly so that Mr. Small stood at the focus of their natural attention.

"Look," Sullivan said. "I don't owe you anything. You owe me plenty. And I wouldn't help you loot Earth—"

"Mr. Sibley. Please. I ask you to think about Doncaster." Small clasped his hands in front of him. "A corporation, as you must know, is more than a single man. It is more than a generation of men. It is a continuing, growing organism, with a greater intelligence and far vaster resources than any individual could command. A corporation, properly administered, might well live forever. But what future could there possibly be, for an immortal, on Earth?"

"Interplanetary Resources tried getting off Earth, Small," Sullivan said harshly. "You know what happened to them."

Leave me alone, Sibley, he thought. I don't need you to tell me what to say.

"Interplanetary Resources," Mr. Small repeated softly. "Yes. Another of our subsidiaries. And an honest effort, Mr. Sibley, until it failed. If Doncaster could have achieved its ends in a straightforward manner, wouldn't that have been much more preferable? But it was not mismanagement nor undercapitalization which made Interplanetary Resources fail, just as it was not a deliberate failure." Mr. Small's eyes grew bitter. "United Metals, Mr. Sibley, is a corporation fully as large as Doncaster. And United Metals, with all its power, lacks the courage

140

to face the night beyond the borders of Earth; though not the greed to cling, cling; like the leech it is, too witless to think of tomorrow, too gluttonous to let a more venturesome entity derive legitimate benefit from legitimate effort. It was when United Metals lobbied through the tariff on off-planet mineral products that Doncaster first set upon the course which has brought us all to this day.

"Think. Think, Mr. Sibley, of what a pioneering venture needs, and think of Doncaster's difficulty, as it was foreseen by some of my predecessors long before you or I or, indeed, anyone alive today was born. It needs people hungry for fertile land, for wealth, for all the things they lack in their old situation. Are there such people on Earth, Mr. Sibley? You know as well as I that there are not—that there will not be, until the day when we all—our descendants, our instruments—even United Metals—even Doncaster—are too poor to support any energetic venture. No, we must have such people *now*, while there is still the venture capital to sustain them. But where are we to get them? Where are we to get a people whom necessity has taught the value of intensive cooperation—who have learned the necessary techniques for the erection of a working industrial economy in a very short space of time? Where can we find these paragons, in this day and age—clever, tough, prepared to meet any possible challenge by Nature or by some other form of life? Where are we to go, if we wish to create not one, but many new markets that will sustain our deathless organism through all the years of the future?"

"You did it on purpose," Sullivan said. "Every bit of it. You created Pluto as a pioneer factory, from start to finish." He looked around the council table again. "You're not going to attack Earth. You never had any intention of attacking Earth. You're forgetting Earth.

You're going out into the stars." It was Allen Sibley's heart that lurched.

"Yes," Hungerford said. "Yessir, Killer! Mankind goes forth to the stars." He stretched his hand out toward Small and the Settlers' Council. "Look at them. Look at them. But, God help me, they're the *only* ones that'll go at all. All along, they've been planning this. Using us all. Even poor Kovacs." He caught back his bitter laugh, and the short, choked sound hung in the room. "Think of what they've done. Think who I'm working for."

"But we *are* going, Mr. MacDonnel, Mr. Sibley. We *are* going," Small whispered. "And if it pleases you to think of our social order in terms of mankind, then you cannot deny that mankind is going." He turned to Sullivan. "None of us here on the Council, nor anyone else of Doncaster's people in the present staff, are of the type to serve in the field." A faint, reflective look came into his eyes. "No," he said in a whisper, "none of us." He put his hands to the top of the long table, as though to push it down out of his way. But that, of course, would have been impossible with so heavy a piece of furniture. Nor was he actually trying. It was only a mannerism.

"We need a man in the field. We have Mr. MacDonnel, but Mr. MacDonnel knows that, like some of us, he dreams better than he does. So we must have someone in charge."

Sullivan looked at Hungerford. The sergeant's head was down, and he swayed listlessly. Sullivan felt a great flash of pity for the man.

Small went on. "We need a ruthless man, because human beings sometimes will not fall of themselves into conformance with a scheme too ramified for them to comprehend. Some of them will find the riches we promised. Some of them will find the danger we trained them to face. We need a man to see to it that nothing

142

of human weakness will impair the function of what will, in the end, be of benefit to them as well as to Doncaster. And at the same time, we need a man capable of understanding that plan. He must feel the inevitable mesh of its workings. He must grasp the slow unfolding of processes that will not mature for decades, for scores of years . . . for centuries." Mr. Small's eyes glowed with the quiet glory of his personal vision. "We must have such a man."

And Allen Sibley looked out at Mr. Small through John L. Sullivan.

"I'll take it away from you," he said. "It'll take time, but I'll have that. And I'll win in the end. I'll take Doncaster away from you and turn it into what *I* think it should be. I don't think anyone should ever have done to them what you've done to these people on Pluto. I don't think anyone should ever talk about anyone the way you talked about Angus MacDonnel just now. I'm warning you, Small—put me where I can plan, and you'll lose Doncaster."

Mr. Small nodded, unsurprised. "I know. But Doncaster will have gone on. I do not like you, Mr. Sibley. But I'm an old man, and what I like will soon matter to no one. Doncaster has lived through me. Doncaster will live through you. And some day, a man as clever as ourselves will take Doncaster from you. But Doncaster will live."

"And people *will* go out to the stars," Hungerford mumbled.

John L. Sullivan came walking into the diner. The place was being closed down. It was open at all only because the spacefield loading crews had to have some place to eat one last meal before they, too, boarded the ships.

Already, the evaluations and judgments were dancing

143

in his mind, constructing the plan that would best ensure their success. The army would go first, to hold the ground if need be, to keep it clear of danger. Then the construction workers among its members would do their work, then the factory hands, and then the women could come in, and the families could begin to clear their fields. Allen Sibley saw exactly how to make all these efforts mesh, how to ensure that everything would go as it ought to.

But John L. Sullivan was the one to begin things.

John L. Sullivan looked across the counter. "Maggie, there's something I have to tell you."